CASSY PRIDE AND THE FEAR DEMON

When a huge demon hunts a small girl, the demon doesn't stand a chance

B. J. Browne

Special thanks to

Michel for your encouragement enthusiasm and support in the writing of this book, also for your comments and suggestions on the story which helped me get this far.

Paulene for your undying enthusiasm, encouragement and the support you've given me. Thank you also for helping with the editing and pointing out errors I had missed.

Oksana for the precious time you spent helping with the editing and for the comments and suggestions you gave.

Table of Contents

Monster in the woods

Cassy Pride lived in a town called Woodhaven, a small place where everyone knows everyone else. She's a young eleven-year-old girl, Indian by ethnic origin although she, and her mum, were born British. Her hair was shoulder length and jet black but shone like it had been polished. Her eyes were a deep, dark brown and her skin a light brown, dad had called it a golden brown, 'golden like your heart sweetheart' he'd say. She was quite small, or petite as mum would affectionately put it, standing at about a hundred and forty centimetres tall.

She wasn't the most popular girl in school, often bullied and a victim of racial insults; although, in all truth, this came from just a small group of bullies, led by Jake, the meanest one of all. She did have friends, but the only ones who were always there for her were, Josh, Rupert and her best friend of all, Sarah.

Her birth father left them when she was just a baby, the man she saw as her dad was an Englishman, who loved her and her mum very much.

This evening was unusual because mum and dad were arguing, they never argued, at least, Cassy had never heard them argue. It was six thirty, and they hadn't really stopped since dad came home from work, apart from a brief quiet spell over dinner time. She sat in her bedroom on the wide windowsill, headphones in and listening to music on her phone, hoping to block out the sounds of her parents, even though they were trying to keep their voices quiet. It was a Thursday evening in January, the sky was clear, star speckled and the moonlight lit the otherwise dark evening. As she looked out of the window, she could see the frost build up on the grass, lit by a street light just the other side of their front garden fence.

Tired of the arguments downstairs she decided to go outside to the front lawn and breathe in the cold but refreshing frosty air. Having turned the music off she put on her wool lined winter coat and boots, she put her torch in her pocket and sneaked out quietly so mum and dad wouldn't hear her. Once outside she crouched down, playing the torchlight over the ground. The frost sparkled and to Cassy, it looked like a million tiny diamonds scattered over the ground, or fairy dust sparkling with magical wonder.

She watched the frost glitter as she slowly moved the torch back and forth, but then, a sound caused her to stop, she stood up and looked around. It sounded like someone shouting, or screaming, but it was distant and she couldn't be sure. She looked past the garden gate, beyond that was the road and past the road, and a little to the right, was a large open grassed area, like a large field where the children often played, especially in the summer. On the other side of the field was the woodland. She stood still, looking and listening, but she couldn't see or hear anything.

Cassy tutted to herself, thinking it must have been her imagination, but then it came again, this time it sounded like a man's scream, followed almost straight away by a woman's scream, but still distant. Her stomach twisted slightly, but deep inside she felt an urge, a strange sort of pull which told her she must go and investigate. She knew it was silly, she was only a young girl after all, and it was darker in the wood where the ground was shaded from most of the moonlight. Nevertheless, something inside told her she must go, something told her it was her duty to go.

She turned and looked towards the house, just in case mum or dad were watching her, but they weren't. She looked back towards the woods again, then another scream, sounding a little closer this time. Cassy's legs seemed to take over and before she knew it, she was out of the gate and crossing the road. A narrow footpath of bare earth ran alongside the open ground and she ran along it, heading straight towards the woods and the place where the screams had come from.

The path led into the woods which seemed to be like a thick wall of trees, quite beautiful in the summer when the leaves covered the branches, but now, stripped of green and in the silvery moonlight they looked almost scary. Cassy felt a strange feeling inside her, one she couldn't quite understand, maybe it was the dark woods making her a little frightened, but it felt different and it made her carry on.

Despite the lack of leaves, the woods were much darker than outside them and eerie shadows danced in the torchlight. Cassy slowed to a walk, her heart was thumping in her chest and she could feel a lump in her throat, the sort of lump that makes your voice a little croaky when you talk. She stopped walking and stood still, trying to figure out where the screams had come from. Then she heard noises that sounded like someone running, and it seemed to come from directly in front of her.

'Run, run for your life!' It was a young woman's voice, and full of fear driven panic. 'RUN.' Then a young woman she recognised fled past her. 'The Devil's coming, run.'

'The Devil?' Cassy questioned, turning to face her but the woman was gone, fear making her run fast.

Cassy turned back towards the inner wood, the way she had been going, and shone the torch ahead. The light shone on the trees but there was nothing to see, then the torch light seemed to just stop a short distance away, like the light was being swallowed up. There was nothing there just a deep blackness, even the trees had gone. Confused, she raised the torch but everything in front of her seemed to have been replaced by a darkness so black it swallowed the light. Her eyes carried on up and then, as if a line had been drawn, the blackness gave way to the star filled, moon lit sky and the silhouetted tree branches. She frowned. 'Weird.' She muttered to herself before looking down a bit at the darkness that blocked the view.

Almost giving up and thinking the hysterical woman screaming of Devils was playing a joke, Cassy decided to go back home. But before she looked back down towards the ground again, two glowing red eyes appeared above her, the red burning like fire. Cassy gasped and as the eyes looked down the fear gripped her, she screamed. It was then that the burning eyes seemed to glow brighter and focus on her. A terrible sound came from whatever it was, a sound like a demon snigger.

Cassy turned and ran, a huge unseen hand swiped where she had been just a moment before, the rush of air from its movement swished through her hair. Her heart thumped so hard in her chest it felt like it was trying to burst out, and an awful panic gripped her stomach.

'I will get you.' It was a deep, frightening voice that seemed to go right through her, but she wasn't sure if it was said out aloud or she had imagined it.

Fortunately, she hadn't wondered too far into the woods, she could hear the monster coming after her, it was so close she could almost feel it at her back. Suddenly she broke out of the cover of the woods, too afraid to stop running she turned her head to look back. Thump, she ran into something, she screamed, hysteria now having gripped her.

'Cassy it's OK, it's me.' She looked up; it was her dad. 'What are you doing?'

'*There's a monster in the woods. It's coming.*' Her panic was clear in her voice and she almost shouted the words.

'Oh Cassy. There aren't any monsters, they don't exist.' Dad said reassuringly. But she wasn't listening properly.

She had turned to look back at the woods, there at the edge she could see those horrible, burning red eyes look at her, but they had dimmed, then they faded and the light was gone.

As she turned back to face dad, she saw the young woman who had run past her, she was now getting close to the far edge of the field and close to a playground. 'She saw it dad, she saw the monster.'

Mum, who was close behind dad caught up with them. 'Cassy, what on earth do you think you're playing at. It's cold, night time and dangerous to go wandering in the woods alone.' Mum sounded cross, but the relief quickly took over and she gave Cassy a big hug.

Cassy was shaking, and nervous having her back to the woods. She turned to look again, pulling away a little from mum's hug. 'I had to help. I had to try anyway.' She said.

'Had to help who? That girl who ran away from you?' Mum asked.

'She was running from the monster, not me.'

Mum's face took on a worried look briefly, then, taking Cassy's hand tight said. 'Let's get back.' Her whole attitude seemed to have changed, but in a subtle way, like she knew something, but she didn't say anything else. She turned and, still holding Cassy's hand tight, started to walk back along the path besides the field towards home.

Dad, who was still trying to figure out how to deal with this, shook his head, as if it would clear his thoughts a bit, then followed. 'This monster business…' He began.

'It was real dad, it was mum. She saw it.' Cassy protested turning slightly and pointing at where the young woman had been last, but she was gone now.

'OK, what did it look like?' Dad asked, trying to play along as contradicting Cassy seemed to wind her up.

'It was huge, black, so black it swallowed the light, and its eyes were like red fire. It was chasing her.' Cassy pointed again to where she saw her last. 'I only went in to the woods because I heard her scream.'

Mum, who would normally have some choice words about not looking for trouble, kept unusually quiet.

'You went into the woods on a cold, frosty night alone because you heard someone scream?' Dad asked, but more as a disbelieving statement.

'If someone needs help, isn't it good to try and help them?' Cassy asked, her voice said she knew she was in trouble.

Dad, who was now walking beside her, put a hand on her shoulder. 'Of course it is sweetheart, but you're still young and sometimes it's better to ask us to help you.'

'You and mum were busy arguing; you wouldn't have listened to me.' Cassy's upset was clear in her voice, in fact she sounded like she was about to cry.

Dad stopped and crouched down, taking Cassy in his arms he gave her a big hug. 'Oh, I'm sorry Cassy. Sometimes grown-ups argue, but we're always there if you need us.'

'Dad.' She then looked back towards the woods again.

'What is it?' He asked.

'I think something horrible's happened. In the woods.'

'OK Cassy, let's get back and talk about it. But it's freezing out here and we need to get back inside. OK.' Mum stated, her voice indicating that she believed what Cassy was saying. Dad looked at her questioningly, but mum just turned to walk back.

The short walk home was filled with insistence that something had happened in the woods, that there was a monster and mum and dad had to believe her. Dad did his best to humour her, but she wasn't fooled. She begged him over and over again to call the police, insisting that something horrible had happened, but couldn't justify this with anything definite. By the time they got home, dad had given in and said he would call the Sergeant, who was a friend of his.

It was nearly quarter to eight before Sergeant Peter Daniels arrived at the house, dad welcomed him in, apologised quietly for calling him out and briefly explained the reason for the call. By now, Cassy knew no-one would believe her, with the possible exception of mum, who had kept quiet. Cassy had become quite hysterical about it all to start with, partly because dad didn't believe what she was saying, although he did seem to believe something had really spooked her, and partly because she now knew monsters existed, and there was one so close to home. But now she had gone quiet too.

'Hello Cassy, your dad tells me something scared you in the woods this evening. Can you tell me about it?' Sergeant Daniels asked in a friendly voice as he crouched down in front of her.

'There's no point!' She exclaimed, tears threatening to fall again.

'OK, I'm sorry to upset you. But, if you've seen something that scared you tonight, I think I should check it out. Dad said that you saw someone running away from a monster in the woods. Can you tell me about the monster you saw?'

'If dad won't believe me, you won't.' She complained.

'Cassy, I…' Dad began, but Sergeant Daniels put his hand up to stop him.

'OK, listen to me Cassy, it's sometimes hard for a grown-up to believe in monsters, but we all believe you saw something that's scared you and I want to help. I promise, if you talk to me, I'll make sure we'll go and look. But first I need an idea of what happened, and what I'm looking for. Will you help me out a bit, please? Tell me what happened, from the beginning?' He asked.

Cassy nodded, although her face said she was unsure about it now. 'I went outside, I like to shine the torch on the frosty ground, it makes the ice twinkle. Then I heard a noise, it sounded like someone screaming, but it sounded so far away I wasn't sure. Then it happened again, a man's scream and then a woman. I don't know why but I had to go and look, so I did. I got to the woods and one of the big girls from school ran past me, shouting at me to run, she said the Devil was coming.' A frightened look passed over her face.

'And that's when you ran from the woods and found your mum and dad?' The sergeant asked sympathetically.

'No.' Her voice sounded like she might be in trouble if she carried on, she lowered her head as if to look at the floor.

'It's OK Cassy, you can tell me. I won't be cross if that's what you're worried about.' He said, as he jotted a few things down on his note pad.

'I wanted to run away, but I thought she was playing a joke on me. I looked the way she had run from, shining my torch in front of me, it was weird because something just stopped the light, just a few metres from me.'

'I'm sorry to interrupt. What do you mean, something stopped the light? I don't understand.' The sergeant asked, frowning.

'It was like there was a wall there, but instead of a wall, it was just black. And the torch couldn't light it. I was… I don't know, I just wanted to know what was stopping the light.'

'And what did you do?'

'I shone the torch up; it was the same until I was looking straight up then I could see the stars. Then these red eyes looked down at me, they were like they were made of red fire. Suddenly they became really bright red and I ran. A horrible, scary voice said it was going to get me.' As she spoke, her words came out faster and faster, until she sounded panicked again.

'OK Cassy, it's OK. Just one more question for now. Do you know who the girl from school is? Just so I can talk to her.' His voice was calm and sympathetic, the look on his face said it was time to stop asking questions now as it was obviously upsetting her.

'I don't know what her name is, I think she lives at the post office.' She said uncertainly.

'Gracie O'Neil?' He questioned. 'You said you heard a man's scream; did you see who that was?'

'No.' She stated bluntly, with a look that said, of course not, on her face.

'It couldn't have been her boyfriend, Shane McAdams, could it?'

'I dunno, I didn't see him.' She looked worried and tearful again.

'OK Cassy, it's alright. Thank you. And, I'm sorry about all the questions.' He smiled at her before turning to face her parents. 'I'll look into it and let you know. I think she could do with a good rest now. If it's alright with you I'll pop in in the morning.' He walked to the door followed by Cassy's parents, opening the door he briefly faced them. Bowing his head he said, 'Nadia, James' as a polite farewell before stepping outside and closing the door behind him.

What they found

It had been a very restless night for Cassy, haunted by nightmares that were terrifying in nature. Every one followed a similar pattern, the black monster chasing her. Some in the woods, others were in the town, one was in her home. The black fearful thing, like a shadow so dark, so black and eyes of fire, always seemed to be after her, but killing everyone who got in its path. Sometimes she'd be walking into town and on the pavements, roads, and the homes where the door was left open, she could see its victims. There was never any blood, never any damage to anything, but the people looked like they had been dried out. Like the ancient mummies she'd seen in a museum.

She was always running from it, always managing to get away. The strangest thing about these dreams was the fact that she never seemed to be scared in them. Nevertheless, she always woke up in a panicky state. Sometimes she'd call out, sometimes she'd scream, but only some of those times were the shouts or screams out aloud, at least, she thought that was the case. A few times mum or dad would come in to comfort her, always commenting that she was shaking and, or sweaty. But for some reason she couldn't understand, she was never afraid, at least, not for herself.

In the last nightmare of the night, she had been in school, the bullies had been picking on her and her friends when it turned up. Rupert had been the first to see it and the fear had paralysed him, he stood there like a statue, but he still managed to scream, Josh and Sarah had followed moments later. When they were taken by the monster, she had run, as was always the case in every one of these horrible dreams. She had run outside but it had cut her off, she was cornered with nowhere to go. Then that deep, awful voice said 'Cassy Pride, you're mine now' and she knew it had been after her all along. All the other people it had killed had just got in its way; she was the real target.

She sat up suddenly while waking, her nightie was sticking to her body as the sweat caused it to cling to her. She was breathing heavily and fast, like a dog panting after a long run. For what felt like ages, but was actually only seconds, she just stared, wide eyed, ahead of her at the wall opposite her bed. Her brain was so desperately trying to catch up with the fact that she was actually awake and not still dreaming.

She shook her head, trying to shake some sense of normality into it, then looked at the alarm clock. '*Eight thirty*! Oh no, I'm going to be late for school.'

As she jumped out of bed, pulled off her nightie then got dressed, she wondered why mum and dad hadn't got her up. Usually, they'd have been shouting at her for still being in bed by now, not that she ever slept in this late on a school day, or at least, rarely did.

Having dressed, she rushed out to use the bathroom, grabbing her school bag as she went. She could hear mum and dad talking downstairs. Oddly, under the circumstances, it occurred to her that they weren't arguing any more, but instead seemed to be talking quietly, hushed voices not meant to be heard. She brushed her teeth and having used the toilet she rushed downstairs.

'I'm sorry. I didn't wake up. I'm going to be late for school, please don't be cross.' She pleaded thinking she was really going to be in trouble. After all, mum and dad took her schooling very seriously.

Both mum and dad came to her, mum gave her a big hug. 'Of course we're not cross with you, after last night I think you could do with the day off school.' She said, using the voice she used when Cassy was ill, sympathetic and caring.

'You went through a lot last night sweetheart, and those bad dreams you were having, we think you need to rest a bit today. Have a chance to get over…' Dad paused, trying to find the right words. '…whatever that was that happened in the woods.'

'We think maybe it would be a good chance to talk with you about it, if you want to.' Mum added.

Cassy was about to say she felt fine, and felt she should go to school when a knock on the door interrupted her thoughts. Dad smiled at her and then went to see who was there. 'Peter, please come in.' She heard him say.

'How's Cassy this morning?' Sergeant Daniels asked quietly, but his voice said something was wrong.

'She's… she seems OK, even got ready for school. She seems more worried about missing school than anything else. Have you found something?' He asked, noting the sergeants concerned look.

His face answered that question for him, he wore a look that suggested that what he'd found had really shaken him up. 'Is Cassy up to talking to me for a bit? There's a few questions I need to ask her.' He said, avoiding the question.

'Um, well, she's literally only just got up, but I guess, if it's important.' Dad said frowning, a questioning worry on his face. 'Come through, she's in the kitchen.' He added, leading the way. 'Cassy, Peter, uh sorry, Sergeant Daniels, is here, he wants to ask you a few questions. Are you up to that?' He asked as they came into the kitchen.

'I suppose so. But I said all I could last night.' Her words were spoken bluntly but politely, although there was less upset than the previous night.

Sergeant Daniels nodded, 'Nadia' he greeted before sitting on a chair and then asked Cassy to sit opposite him, on a chair she was standing by. Cassy did, then turning to mum asked. 'Can I have a drink please mum?'

'Of course, darling.' Mum replied and set about getting her a glass of orange juice.

'OK Cassy. I know you told me what happened last night, but I need to double check a couple of things. Can you tell me, how far did you go into the woods?' Sergeant Daniels asked.

'Not far.' She replied.

Sergeant Daniels looked a little frustrated, he tightened his lips a moment before speaking again. 'Can you be a little more… I mean, was it two metres, ten metres a hundred metres, just round about.'

Cassy looked at mum, then dad. She was picking up on the sergeant's frustration and feeling a little worried in case she was in trouble. 'I, I don't know, just a… ten, twenty metres maybe.' She looked at dad again, then back at the Sergeant. 'Not very far.'

'OK, are you sure you didn't see anything else? You were quite frightened last night, have you remembered anything at all?'

'No.'

'This monster, can you tell me again what you saw.'

'It was just dark, black like a shadow that made the light disappear. It had red eyes.' She started to feel very uncomfortable now.

'You said its eyes were like fire last night.' He said.

'Yes. They got lighter when it saw me.'

'You said it chased you, is that right?'

'Yes.'

'OK, James, Nadia, did you see anything at all? I mean, Cassy says it chased her, but she wasn't far into the woods. With eyes like fire, I would imagine you should have seen something.' His question was more like a statement.

'No. Peter what have you found, or found out? You seem quite on edge this morning.' Dad asked.

'Yes, yes I apologise, it's been a long, strange night. I spoke to Gracie O'Neil last night. She um, well, she was in shock so the doctor said when we called him out.

'She seemed to confirm Cassy's story that the Devil chased her. She and her boyfriend, Shane McAdams, had been in the woods, to the clearing, you know, the open area where the youngsters go and hang out or camp in the summer. She claims the Devil rose out of the ground like a giant shadow…' While he paused, he squeezed his eyes tight shut before relaxing and stretching his brow. He moved his head from side to side, like a slow shake then said. '…she said it had eyes of red fire.'

'I told you. See dad, I wasn't lying. It's true, it was real. Just like I said.' Cassy said in a defensive tone.

'OK, Cassy, calm down, I didn't say you were lying.' Dad reasoned.

'To start with I did wonder if the girls were playing some joke, a prank or something. I mean, the story is a bit, well, far-fetched, out there. But…' The Sergeant paused and looked almost embarrassed.

Dad frowned, looking at him questioningly. 'What?'.

'Well, early this morning I had a panicked call from Rose McAdams, Shane's mum; he didn't come home last night.

'So, I took a couple of officers with me to search the woods…' He stopped again, this time he seemed lost in his thoughts.

'And? What did you find? Or didn't you?' Mum asked.

'He was dead, dried like that mummy we saw in the museum last year, wasn't he.' Cassy stated, as if she was thinking out aloud, with a faraway look on her face.

They all looked at her, mum and dad looked surprised, but Sergeant Daniels looked shocked. 'Cassy!' Mum said, sounding a little cross at her daughter's rather dark comment.

'How...' Sergeant Daniels began, but stopped for a moment. '... could you know that?' He finished.

'It was in my dreams. I... dreamt it, sort of.' Cassy looked at the Sergeant, then from mum to dad. Then suddenly she stood up and ran upstairs to her bedroom leaving the grown-ups looking at each other in questioning surprise.

Cassy sat on her bed, she felt as confused as Sergeant Daniels, mum and dad did. How could she have known about Shane? Why were her dreams telling her what this monster did? But the thing that frightened her most was the fact that, in her dreams, the monster was after her. Could that be true too? And if so, why her? She was just a young girl, what could it want her for?

As lots of questions flowed through her mind, she lay down, glad for the fact that she didn't have to go to school today. She did have a strong feeling that she had to do something, but had no idea as to what that might be. Her head was all jumbled up with so many thoughts, and the images of the events the night before filled her memories making everything seem so confusing.

She lay there trying to make sense of everything for quite some time, then a knock on the door made her jump. 'Are you OK sweetheart?' Dad said as he opened the door.

She looked up, both mum and dad stood in the doorway. 'Yeah, I think so.' But the look on her face said otherwise.

Both mum and dad came over and sat on the bed, when Cassy sat up, mum gave her a hug. 'Do you want to talk about these dreams you had? Or what happened last night?' She asked.

'It must be very frightening for you, we're here if you need to talk, about anything. You know that, right?' Dad added.

'I know.' She replied. 'It's just...' But she couldn't find the words to finish the sentence.

'It's what?' Dad asked sympathetically. But mum looked at him and lightly closed her eyes and shook her head as if to gently say 'Don't press it too hard.'

'I don't know how I could have known. I mean, known what happened to Shane. How could I have known that?' Then she looked past them, as if looking through them. 'What if the other things in my dreams come true too?'

'I don't know darling, but we're here for you, you know that.' Mum said.

'Maybe, just maybe, talking about the dreams might help. But we won't push you into it. Only when you're ready, and when you are, we'll be there to listen.' Dad added.

Cassy then looked at them. 'Does the school know I'm not going in today?' She asked.

Mum smiled at her. 'Yes, we've called them.'

The need to know

Mum and dad had sat with her for about half an hour that morning, gently encouraging her to talk about her dreams, but she couldn't. To her, if *she* couldn't make sense of them, then how could mum and dad? Although, inside she wanted to tell them all her thoughts, feelings and fears the dreams and events had left her with, but she just couldn't, or maybe it was that she didn't know how.

She hadn't been able to face breakfast, she ate a little lunch but it was hard to eat much. It was now three forty-five and the day was already starting to go dim outside. The clear skies had become cloudy, although light cloud, which meant the lack of sunshine was making it darken sooner than the last few days.

Most of the afternoon had been spent sitting at her windowsill. Her eyes kept on being drawn to the woodland, her mind to the monster that roamed there. For some very strange reason, she had the urge to go to the woods again, to find this monster, but of course, that was crazy. Nevertheless, something inside her was trying to pull her that way.

'Cassy.'

'Hey Cassy, down here.' The calls made her jump a little as she was pulled from her thoughts.

She looked down to the front lawn, Sarah, Rupert and Josh were waving at her. She beckoned them with her hands and then headed for the door. Downstairs, mum and dad greeted her like they hadn't seen her for days.

'Is it OK for Sarah, Josh and Rupert to come in?' She asked, but barely broke her stride as she headed for the front door.

'Uh, yes, OK.' Mum said as Cassy passed through the kitchen-diner at a pace.

She reached the door and opened it. 'Hi guys.' She greeted.

'Are you OK?' Josh said, quickly getting it in before the others could.

'Miss said you were ill today, that's why you weren't in school.' Sarah quickly got in.

'I'm… yeah, I'm OK. Not ill really.' Cassy said awkwardly.

'Why weren't you in school then?' Rupert asked.

'It's complicated.' She replied. 'Come in, mum said it's OK.'

The three friends came in, obviously pleased to see her, and see her well.

'Hello, Sarah, Josh, Rupert. How was school today?' Mum greeted.

'Hello. School was OK.' Rupert replied.

'Hello, Mrs Pride, hello, Mr Pride.' Sarah said.

'Hello.' Josh added.

'You going upstairs?' Dad asked.

Cassy shrugged then looked at her friends. 'My bedroom or the living room?' she asked.

'Bedroom.' Sarah said in a definite way with a smile on her face.

'Bedroom.' Cassy said in response to her dad's question. She then led her friends upstairs.

'Well, they seem to have cheered her up a bit.' Mum said in a pleased way.

As soon as the four friends went into Cassy's bedroom and the door was closed, Rupert said, sounding very excited. 'Have you heard what everyone's saying?

'They say something terrible happened in the woods last night.' Josh eagerly said, almost before Rupert had finished.

'Some are even saying there's a monster there. As if a monster would come here.' Sarah added, grinning.

Cassy looked down for a moment, then gave her friends a brave, forced smile before walking over to her bed and sitting down. She didn't say a word.

'Hey, what's up with you? Usually, you'd get all talky about things like that.' Sarah asked disappointedly.

'All talky? That's not even a real word.' Josh said poking fun at her.

''Tis so.' Sarah argued.

'Hey, Cassy, are you OK?' Rupert asked sounding concerned.

Sarah and Josh looked over at Cassy and all excitement left them. The three friends then went over to join her sitting on the bed.

'Something terrible did happen in the woods last night. That's why I wasn't in school today. I saw it… sort of.' Cassy said, her tone very serious, the last part a little unsure.

'Hey, what was it?' Sarah asked, full of concern for her best friend.

'Some kids are saying that someone was killed there. Did you see a dead person?' Josh asked, unable to hide his morbid excitement.

'*Josh*!' Sarah said, sounding cross, while Rupert smirked, trying not to laugh.

Cassy looked at Josh then at Rupert, her face said she wasn't impressed, then, softening her look she looked at Sarah. But she found herself lost for words.

'Hey Cassy, I was only messing about. It's only kids making up stories.' Josh said looking a bit embarrassed. 'Sorry.' He added after a second or two.

'It's OK. After all, nothing like that ever happens here, right? Only last night it did, and I've got this feeling it's only just begun.' Cassy said.

The three friends looked at each other wide eyed and then back at Cassy. Rupert swallowed hard, making a quiet gulping noise, all three were silent, waiting for her to continue. She closed her eyes and lowered her head, then took in a deep breath and let it out in a slow blow. She then looked up at her friends, each one for a second at a time which was just long enough to let them know she was serious.

'This is so scary; my wits are silly.' Rupert said, being deadly serious.

Josh burst out laughing, he laughed so hard he fell off the bed and onto the floor. Sarah, who was trying to keep a straight face couldn't hold it in once Josh was on the floor. With two of them laughing, the funny side of it all sank into Cassy who then started to giggle.

'It's… it's…' Josh tried to correct him, but with the laughter he could hardly get one word out.

'Scared out of my wits, or...' Cassy said, pausing with her giggling.

'Scared silly.' Sarah added, finishing off Cassy's sentence.

'Stoopid.' Josh finished.

At this, Cassy couldn't hold it in any longer and the contagious laughter exploded out of her. After a few seconds of looking embarrassed, even Rupert saw the funny side and the room was filled with the sound of very happy, very amused children.

Downstairs, mum and dad looked at each other and smiled. 'Seems like what she really needed were her friends.' Dad said.

'It's so good to hear her laugh.' Mum said with a smile. 'Why is children's laughter so contagious?' She asked, not meaning it to be answered. With that she gave a little giggle.

'This will really do her some good, she's seemed so moody all day. Not that I can blame her of course.' Dad added.

'Maybe we should invite Sarah, Josh and Rupert to dinner tonight. Maybe this is exactly what Cassy needs. We can give their parents a call, just to make sure it's alright. What do you say, James?'

'I think it would be a great idea.' He replied, then leaned over and gave her a kiss. 'I can take them back later.'

Mum smiled and nodded her agreement.

Back upstairs the laughter eased, Cassy was the first to stop. Her thoughts became serious again, although the lightened mood had lifted her spirits a bit.

'So come on, tell us everything.' Josh said after he calmed himself down and sat on the bed again.

'Yeah, what happened? Must have been serious if you got the day off school.' Sarah added.

'Well, I went out to the front lawn last night and heard a scream from the woods, so I went to check it out.' Cassy began.

'You went to the wood on your own, at night?' Rupert asked in amazement.

'It wasn't that late, and the moon was bright so it wasn't that dark. Anyway, I got to the woods, I only went in a very short way, thank God. Then what's her name, Gracie, from the post office came running past me shouting at me to run saying the Devil was coming. Then I saw…' She stopped while she tried to think of how to describe it.

'Saw what?' Sarah asked.

'It was, I don't know, like a very black shadow, it was huge and swallowed up the light from my torch. I looked up and saw eyes like red burning flames.'

'What did you do?' Rupert asked, eyes wide open and his voice a little wobbly.

'I ran like hell. Mum and dad had noticed I'd gone so came to look for me, I ran into them just out of the woods. The monster, whatever it is, chased me, but didn't leave the wood to get me. It was so scary.

'Dad called the police. Sergeant Daniels came over this morning and said they found a body in the woods.'

'Who was it? Gracie?' Josh asked.

'No, her boyfriend Shane, he was dried up like a mummy.' Cassy said.

'You're joking! I saw Shane yesterday in town.' Sarah said, amazement on her face.

Cassy was about to answer, but Rupert, looking quite frightened, asked. 'What was it? Is it still there?'

'I don't know, Rupert. But last night I had lots of dreams about it, it kept chasing me everywhere I went. It killed everyone in its way leaving just dried-up bodies after. That's the scary bit, I knew what it had done to Shane. But what's spooked me most was that in my dreams, it said it was after me.'

'That is scary, but it was just a dream.' Sarah said, trying to be comforting.

'I'm not sure it was, Sarah. My head is full of thoughts, feelings I don't understand. It's like, I don't know, like I should know what to do, like it's up to me to stop it.' Cassy said, looking straight ahead as if in a trance.

'Don't be daft Cassy, you're a kid, why you when there's grown-ups to deal with it? Anyway, whatever's out there, I'm sure it's not the Devil or a real monster. Monsters don't exist. Do they?' Rupert's voice quavered and his face suddenly looked frightened again as he asked the question.

'CASSY.' Mum called from downstairs.

Cassy went to the door and opened it. 'Yeah mum.'

'Ask your friends if they would like to stay for dinner. Dad said he'd take them home after.'

Cassy looked at her friends on the bed but she didn't need to say anything as they had all heard and were nodding enthusiastically. Cassy smiled. 'Yes please mum, thanks.'

'You're welcome darling.' Mum called back. 'I'll give their parents a call, just to make sure it's OK.'

'Thank you.' Cassy said, and she couldn't help the huge smile spread across her face.

The four friends talked about monsters, Cassy's dreams and such like, but gradually, Cassy began to go quiet. Her mind was stuck on the thing in the woods and questions her dreams had made her ask. What if this monster did want her? Why did she have such a strong feeling that she was the one who had to do something about it? And, if that was the case, how could she, a young nobody, possibly beat it?

'Yoo-hoo, earth to Cassy.' Sarah's voice broke her trance.

Cassy looked up, but all three friends were looking at her having gone quiet. 'I've got to go back into the woods.' She stated.

'What?!' Rupert said, wide eyed.

'You nuts?!' Josh added, shocked surprise filling his voice.

Sarah looked at her, shaking her head. 'Cassy, you can't. If it killed Shane, you don't stand a chance.'

'I have too. I need to know.'

'Need to know what?' Sarah was starting to sound a little desperate and panicky. Josh and Rupert just looked at her as if she'd lost her mind.

'That's the strange thing, I don't really know, but there's an answer there, in the woods, somewhere. Maybe I just need to see what it is. Will you guys come with me?' Cassy had a faraway look on her face again.

'I'm not going near those woods in the dark.' Rupert said.

'Nor me.' Josh added, backing Rupert up.

'I thought boys were supposed to be the brave ones.' Sarah grinned before turning back. 'But they do have a point, it's dangerous Cassy.'

'Well, I'm going, tomorrow during the day. I can't explain it, but I have to.'

Sarah took in a deep breath. 'OK, we can't let you go alone. I'll come with you.' She reluctantly agreed.

'You girls are crazy.' Rupert grumbled.

'Nuts.' Josh repeated.

Sarah then made a fist and, holding it sideways on, held it out in front of her. 'One in.' She said.

The boys sighed in defeat. Cassy followed Sarah, holding her fist out in front of her but on top of Sarah's. Josh and Rupert did the same, one fist above another. 'All in.' They said together.

Back to the woods

Saturday morning arrived pretty much in the same way as Friday morning had, suddenly waking from a dream about the monster, and again, the whole night had been filled with such dreams. The only difference was that last night's dreams had felt different, but in ways Cassy couldn't really describe, not even to herself. She had woken a few times, sometimes shouting, sometimes screaming and either mum or dad had come to comfort her, but she never felt afraid. There had been a difference in the monster though, somehow it had been bigger, stronger, more frightening, this was very strange as Cassy had not felt any fear of it, neither in her dreams or on waking.

She got out of bed and walked to her window, a small flurry of snow had lightly dusted the ground outside sometime during the night, but this was not what she looked at. The woods just a short distance away seemed to hold a mix of fascination and dread, but the dread was not so much for her, or her friend's safety, but something else. Maybe it was just knowing that there was a monster there.

Sergeant Daniels had called in the night before just to check up on how Cassy was. He had said that the police were still at a loss as to exactly what had happened in the woods. The body they had found had indeed been that of Shane McAdams, but how it had ended up like it was, was a mystery. There had been a full-scale search of the woods during the day but nothing had been found. He said he hoped this was just a one-off thing and the descriptions give of this monster had been due to the dim moonlight casting unusual shadows. Cassy had kept quiet, but both mum and dad knew she was not fooled, or convinced, by the police answer to the case.

Sarah, Josh and Rupert had gone home around eight o'clock. Dad had taken them home by car which they had been thankful of, it had been cold and they were a bit frightened by the whole thing, neither one of them wanting to walk about in the dark outside. In the privacy of Cassy's bedroom, they had hatched their secret plan for the day. They would meet up at Cassy's house, then go out to play once they had got themselves ready. It was unlikely that mum and dad would think anything of it, the cold weather hardly ever kept them in. They would use a different route into the woods, one where Cassy's mum and dad wouldn't see, that is if they were watching.

Cassy really didn't know what she was hoping, or dreading, to find, or indeed, if they did find something, what she planned to do. All she could be sure of was that she had to go, she just couldn't shake the strong feeling inside that somehow it was her duty, that somehow it was down to her to find this thing and… and what she really didn't know.

She walked back to the bed and sat on the edge. The clock told her it was eight forty-two, for a moment it struck her as being a little odd that she had woken at about the same time as the day before. But it was even more odd that twice in a row she had slept later than usual, even at the weekends she would normally be awake by seven. But these were passing thoughts, her mind was too concerned with the day ahead.

Having got dressed she went downstairs. Mum was in the kitchen. 'Good morning.' She greeted with a smile.

'Morning, mum.' She returned the smile as she sat down.

'How are you this morning? Dad, and I are a little worried about you; these nightmares you're having… Well, it's been two nights in a row. Do you want to talk about them yet?'

'I don't really know what to say mum. It's just dreams of that monster, it is weird though, I never seem to be scared of it, only scared for other people.' Cassy said, but by the look on her face she could have been talking to herself.

Mum looked at her and raised a questioning eyebrow. 'You're waking up in a panic Cassy.' Mum said as a statement rather than a questioning invite to talk.

'That's why it's so hard to talk about it mum, you won't understand.'

'Hey, I thought I heard you.' Dad said as he came into the kitchen-diner from the living room. He kissed Cassy on her forehead then asked. 'How are you this morning?'

'I'm OK.' She replied.

'Slept in late again. Those dreams you're having must be making you tired.' He smiled a sympathetic smile.

'I guess, a little.' She shrugged.

'Well, if it carries on much longer, I think it might be a good idea to get you in with someone you can talk about it to, perhaps see the doctor.' He suggested.

Cassy was about to reply but mum got in first. 'That's maybe not a bad idea darling. You're not sleeping properly and it's obviously bothering you.'

'Honestly, it's OK.' But Cassy's frown and the faraway look on her face didn't convince her parents.

Mum put a glass of orange juice down for her and then brought over a bowl and spoon, a packet of cereal and a jug of milk. She then smiled at Cassy in a way that said she didn't believe it was OK, but would talk about it again.

'So, what time's the gang turning up?' Dad asked, changing the subject.

'About ten, but knowing Rupert and Josh that could be eleven.' She grinned.

'Got anything planned?' Mum asked, smiling.

'Nothing really. We might go out later, I don't want to be inside again today. Maybe see if there's any more snow in town.'

'Snow?' Dad questioned.

'A light dusting fell last night.' Mum said, she then turned her attention back to Cassy. 'But I doubt there'll be more in town than here.' The look on her face said sorry to break the bad news.

'No, you're probably right.' Cassy agreed, then turned her attention to having breakfast.

'Just keep clear of the woods, OK. Until they know what's happening there, it's better to be safe than sorry.' Dad put his hand on her shoulder as he spoke. He then nodded as if an agreement had been made before turning to go back into the living room.

It was five to ten when Sarah turned up. 'Hii.' She said, making the 'i' sound stretch out when Cassy opened the door.

Cassy invited her in with a hand gesture. 'Josh and Rupert not with you?'

'Haven't seen them yet. Probably still in bed.' Sarah giggled a bit at her making fun of them.

'I wonder if Rupert's wits are still silly.' Cassy said giving a little giggle of her own.

'Morning Sarah.' Mum said from the kitchen.

'Good morning Mrs Pride.' She greeted.

'Looks cold out.' Mum said just as a polite comment.

'It is a bit, but not too bad.' Sarah replied, grinning at Cassy.

'C'mon, let's go upstairs.' Cassy said, then they both headed up.

It was about ten past ten before Josh and Rupert turned up together. Dad let them in and they found their own way up to Cassy's room. They chatted for a while and planned what they were going to do, although that part was fairly brief as they didn't really know. It might just turn out to be a walk in the woods or they might find the monster's den. Whichever the case may be, exactly what they would do depended on what happened. After all, how do you plan for that which you don't know?

After a while, Cassy got her warm, wool lined boots and coat on, she got her warm gloves and put a torch in her pocket.

'Why do you need a torch, its daytime?' Josh asked in a whisper.

'Just in case.' Cassy answered.

'In case of what?' Rupert followed up.

Cassy and Sarah looked at him as if he was stupid. 'In case we need it.' Cassy sarcastically said.

Both Rupert and Josh looked a little confused, but decided not to ask any more questions. Once everyone was wrapped and ready to go, they went downstairs.

'You off out now?' Mum asked as they tried to quietly get to the front door.

'Yes mum.' Cassy replied.

'How long you planning on being out? I'm just thinking, I could make some toasted sandwiches for lunch. Your favourites.'

'Ooh, yes please. Can…' Cassy enthusiastically began.

'Yes, Cassy, Sarah Josh and Rupert are welcome.' Mum said.

'Thanks mum.'

'Thankyou Mrs Pride.' Sarah, Josh and Rupert said, although not quite together.

'You kids are more than welcome. About One?' She asked, but it was meant more as a statement.

'See you at one.' Cassy said with a beaming smile. They then all left the house.

Ten minutes later they had got out of view of the house and onto another path leading into the woods. 'OK, stay close and keep a close watch.' Cassy said taking charge.

'What are we watching out for exactly. A monster?' Rupert said sounding a bit worried.

'Anything not supposed to be there. Anything that can give us a clue about the monster. Most of all the monster itself.' Cassy said sounding a bit fed up with the questions.

Rupert gulped making a noise. Sarah just looked at him and slowly shook her head. 'Do you want to hold my hand, Rupert?' She said, holding her hand out and smiling to let him know she was teasing him.

'Ha ha.' Rupert replied, but inside he was very tempted to take her up on the offer.

As they slowly and carefully walked through the woods they were silent. Cassy was concentrating, she could feel something deep inside. 'Can you feel that?' She asked in a whisper.

'Feel what? I can't feel anything.' Sarah replied.

'Nor me.' Josh confirmed. Rupert just raised his eyebrows and shook his head.

'Something… I don't know.' Cassy said in reply to Sarah's question. 'Let's go that way, to the clearing.' She said quietly.

They carried on silently as before. The feeling inside Cassy seemed to grow, like the sort of feeling you get in the stomach when you know you're in trouble, or you want something really badly and can't wait. She started to think of the clearing, just in case it was due to expecting something being there, but thinking about it made no difference. The feeling seemed to get stronger the closer they got.

'There it is.' Josh whispered, his voice showing not only a bit of excitement, but also a little afraid.

They stopped and looked at Cassy. 'What now?' Sarah asked in a whisper.

'Go down there.' Cassy said bluntly, the feeling was now like a pit in her stomach, but at least it seemed to have stopped growing, or so she thought.

They carefully made their way, then Rupert screeched.

'What?' Cassy called.

'Down there.' Rupert said pointing a finger.

'Ah, gross.' Josh put his left hand over his mouth while pointing in the same direction as Rupert.

Sarah gasped and stepped backwards; panic was very clear on her face. Cassy stepped forward to see as she hadn't spotted what the others were distressed about. Then she saw, at the edge of the clearing were three bodies, they were fully clothed but their faces and hands said they were dried out, just as she'd seen in her dreams. In fact, this was just like a dream she'd had, but she couldn't really remember it. She only seemed to recall it as it happened, almost as if this was a dream.

'Cassy.' Sarah said, sounding very distressed. Cassy was just standing there, staring at the bodies in a trance. 'Cassy, come on.'

'I've got to go down.' Cassy said, then she started to walk down the small path that led to the clearing.

Opposite the path she was on was another path, wider and more used. This path led out to the field opposite Cassy's house. Almost deaf to the pleas of her friends she continued down until she reached the bottom. It wasn't a steep slope, just a gentle downward path, the clearing itself was like a shallow bowl which flattened off at the bottom. It was a perfect place to set up a tent in the summer, which is what some did. The makings of a fire pit was in the centre, blackened stones and charcoal in the middle, sparkling with the frost and speckled with the slight snow dusting.

The other three friends, both afraid to leave Cassy alone, and also afraid to go without her, but as she seemed to be the only one of them who had any idea what was happening, they followed her down. They clung close to each other but moved quickly to catch up with Cassy.

Cassy had stopped, she looked down at the bodies, then turned to look around her.

'What is it, Cassy?' Sarah asked seeing the look on her face.

'Come on, let's get out of here.' Josh stated, hoping to spur everyone into moving.

'This gives me the creeps.' Rupert was pale in the face, obviously scared. Josh and Rupert had spoken almost at the same time.

'This is where the monster is. I can feel it.' Cassy then turned to face the others. 'Can't *you* feel it?'

As if the others hadn't even mentioned any concerns, she walked into the centre of the clearing. The pit in her stomach seemed to suddenly increase and run through her body. Like an electrical current which spread fear throughout her, but it was more like nervous tension rather than raw fear. Fear was what her friends obviously felt, but this only registered with her now as she turned to look at them.

Suddenly, like a thunderbolt, the tension caught up with her and the need to get out of the woods was strong. 'This way, run.' She said heading for the larger path leading out to the field. 'Quick, run.' Her voice sounded slightly panicked and she had raised her voice almost to a shout.

The other three didn't need anything else to get them moving. The four of them ran through the woods. Cassy was now feeling quite afraid and convinced that there was something, the monster, chasing them. Her heart pounded in her chest and she had a lump in her throat which made her feel slightly sick. Behind her, Josh, Sarah and Rupert were running as fast as they could. Rupert was in a state of sheer terror, feeling like something was snapping at his heels. Sarah was convinced that Cassy had seen something coming, and that was why she suddenly went from wanting to look around to running away. Josh just wanted to get out of the woods, he was scared, but unsure of whether it was the bodies which had freaked him out, or something else.

Cassy saw it just before she ran into it. Unable to stop she tripped and landed heavily on the woodland floor. The thump as she hit the ground knocked the wind out of her. Josh who was the next behind her tried to stop, not having seen what Cassy had fallen over, he too tripped and fell. Fortunately, both Sarah and Rupert had more warning and managed to stop. As they approached to offer help Sarah gasped, she wanted to scream but somehow couldn't, also, deep inside her, she held a need to keep herself from doing that in front of the boys.

Rupert caught up just moments after, he too gasped, then shrieked as a sense of panic rushed through him. There on the floor was another body, this one was not only dried out, like the others they'd seen, but also damaged, as if it had been dropped through the trees. Josh got himself up and quickly moved over to help Cassy who was struggling to her feet. Rupert was just staring at the body on the floor, while Sarah moved around to help Cassy, but was trying to take the widest path so as not to get too close to it.

'You, ok?' She asked Cassy.

'Yeah, I think so.' She replied.

'You ok, Josh?' Sarah asked.

'Hurt my knee.' He said, holding it with both hands.

'You ok to walk? We need to get out of the woods, we need to tell the police. Oh no, mum and dad's going to kill me, they told me not to go near the woods.' Cassy said as she got up, she looked worried as she spoke.

'There's a dead body on the floor.' Rupert whimpered, but stating it as if the others might not have noticed.

'We know.' Cassy, Sarah and Josh all said together.

Cassy and Sarah helped Josh, there was a bit of blood on his trousers over the knee and he limped slightly. 'Let's get out of here.' He said in a voice that sounded pleading. He looked in disgust at the body on the floor and was feeling disgusted as it was what he'd tripped up on.

Once they had brushed themselves off, they quickly got out of the woods, it only took a minute or two as they had gone pretty far running so fast. Once clear of the woods, they then headed along the path towards Cassy's house. They were all worried about what their parents were going to say.

Breaking the news

They rushed into the house like a mob, causing mum to jump at the suddenness of their entrance.

'Mum, I need to tell you something, dad too.' Cassy blurted out, quite breathless after all the running.

'What is it?' She asked, then she noticed the blood on Josh's trouser knee. 'Josh, what have you done? Are you OK?'

'Just hurt my knee a bit.' He replied sheepishly.

Just then, dad came in from the living room. 'You've been in the woods, haven't you?' He said looking a little cross and looking at the bits in Cassy and Josh's hair and clothes.

'Dad, I can explain.' Cassy said defensively. 'I had to, but I knew you wouldn't have let me.'

'You had to?' Mum said backing dad up and in a voice that said she couldn't believe what her daughter had just said. 'Why did you have too? We told you not to go to the wood Cassy, it's not safe.'

'Cassy, there's been a… well...' Dad began.

'Murder.' Cassy said finishing off dad's sentence.

'Not just one, Mr and Mrs Pride.' Sarah added, looking at each of Cassy's parents as she spoke.

'There's four more bodies there now.' Rupert almost shouted the words.

'Rupert.' Josh's voice said he shouldn't have said that, not that they were going to keep it a secret.

'What!' Now mum did sound cross.

'You've found four more people, dead, in the woods?' Dad asked, as if there was a need for it to actually be said. 'I'm going to call Peter.' As he spoke, he moved over to the phone. 'After, young lady, we're going to talk.' He added looking directly at Cassy.

'Josh come here; I'd better take a look at that knee.' Mum said. Josh moved over to a chair and sat down, as he pulled his trouser leg up carefully, mum added. 'So, what happened to your leg?'

'I fell, tripped over.' He didn't really want to tell her too many details as neither she nor Mr Pride sounded happy with them.

'Tripped over what?'

'A dead person.' Rupert stated, then realised he shouldn't have spoken. He stretched his lower lip, as if to say sorry to his friends, and oops for saying anything.

'Mum, please don't be cross. I know it sounds crazy and I know I disobeyed you and dad, but I had too. My dreams…' She stopped and, looked down in silence.

A worried look briefly flashed over mum's face. 'OK Cassy, we'll talk about it when dads finished on the phone.' Her voice had softened, almost as if she understood.

It was at this time that dad spoke to Sergeant Daniels. It was quite a brief chat where dad asked him if he could come over as there was something Cassy needed to tell him. Not that anyone was really listening.

Mum got a damp cloth and the first aid box and started to clean Josh's knee. 'It's not too bad, just skinned it a bit.' She said after cleaning the blood away. 'I'm just going to give it a clean with a sterile wipe, I think a bit of antiseptic cream and a plaster will do the trick.'

Having finished on the phone dad said that Sergeant Daniels was coming over, but he wanted to hear the story first. Mum suggested he let her finish with Josh's leg first to which he agreed. He waited patiently. After finishing with Josh, mum asked if anyone else was hurt, to which they all said they weren't.

'OK Cassy, you first. Tell us why you had to go to the woods.' Mum asked before dad could say anything.

'It's my dreams, it's like, I don't know, like they're telling me something. It feels more than just dreams. But please, Sarah, Josh and Rupert, they didn't really know much about it. It's me you should be cross with not them.' Cassy looked at her parents with a pleading look on her face.

Mum moved over to Cassy and gave her a hug. 'It's not so much that we're cross darling, but we are worried about you. Your friends too. Whatever's going on in the woods, it's dangerous, and you're so young, all of you.' As she said the last part, she looked at Sarah, Josh and Rupert. Dad gave her a look that said she was being too soft, but mum just frowned, giving a slight shake of her head, as a way of saying to ease off and be calm.

'Mum, dad, I know it doesn't make sense, it doesn't to me either, but I feel…' She paused, realising she didn't really know how to say it, even if she understood it well enough, it was just too confusing. 'In my dreams, this monster is after me, everyone else it gets are just in its way. The other night, I had this feeling, like I had to go to the woods, I didn't know why but I had to. Like something was making me go.'

'How do you mean; something was making you go? How?' Dad asked.

'I don't know, really, I suppose it was a bit like I was being pulled there, but in my mind. Like I had to go and help. Then there's my dreams, I think they're trying to tell me something, I just don't know what.'

'Sweetheart, I don't think dreams try and tell you things, they're more, well, they say dreams are just your mind making sense of things that have happened, a bit like a computer, checking all the files, saving some things in your memory, putting others in the recycle bin. That's why they often don't make sense, they're jumbled up bits of information.' Dad tried to reason.

'That's just it dad, they weren't jumbled up, they all made sense, but I have to work out what the sense means.' Cassy was starting to look and sound frustrated now.

Dad was about to say something when there were a few flashes of blue light coming from outside. Dad went to the window which looked out onto the front lawn. 'Ah, Peter's here. Listen, you kids have got to tell him what happened in the woods today. It's important.'

'We will.' Cassy said. The others nodded in agreement.

Dad went to the door and as soon as he saw Sergeant Daniels through the frosted glass pane in the door, he opened it. 'Peter, please, come in. That was quick.'

'Hello James. I came straight over; you sounded like it was urgent.' He said.

'Yes, it's uh, this whole business is quickly becoming an emotional rollercoaster.'

'What's up, you do seem a bit shaken.' Sergeant Daniels said, full of concern.

'I think the kids had better explain it to you.' Dad answered.

'The kids?' He questioned as they walked through to the kitchen. 'Oh, hello Rupert Josh, Sarah. I didn't realise you were here.'

'Hello, Sergeant Daniels.' Sarah politely greeted, but her voice was a bit blank.

'Hello.' Josh and Rupert said.

'OK, so I understand you wanted to tell me something, Cassy. Or was it all of you?' Sergeant Daniels said as a way of opening up the conversation.

'We found something in the woods today.' Cassy said a bit sheepishly, expecting to get told off about it.

'You went back into the woods, after the, well, what happened there the other night? You know we've been trying to stop people going in there don't you?' Sergeant Daniels was firm but not angry sounding.

'Yes sir. But we found four more bodies. Three were just dried up like poor Shane was, the other was… hurt, I mean broken.' Cassy said, meanwhile, Sarah, Josh and Rupert stayed quiet and looked a bit awkward.

'Four more bodies?' He questioned in a tone of disbelief. 'Can you tell me where they are?' He asked. 'Hang on. You say one was broken? Do you mean damaged?'

'Yes, damaged. There were three at the clearing, the other one is on the path leading from the clearing to the field.' She said, pointing in the direction of the field across the road as she mentioned it.

'OK, I'll get someone to come with me to take a look.' Sergeant Daniels was frowning as he spoke and looked as if he was in deep thought.

'Sir, Cassy thinks the monster is at the clearing.' Josh said uncomfortably.

Sergeant Daniels looked at Cassy with raised eyebrows. 'You think the monster is at the clearing?' He repeated, but as a question. Although he had no idea what could have done what happened to Shane McAdams, but in his mind, monsters were still fiction, or a way of describing evil people.

'I'm sure of it, I could feel it.' Cassy answered.

'If you were all there, at the clearing, did you see, or feel anything? Sergeant Daniels asked.

Sarah, Josh and Rupert all shook their heads. 'But it was very scary there, and something killed those people.' Rupert argued.

'OK, well I'll go and check this out and come back later. In the meantime, I need you to promise me you'll stay out of the woods for the time being. There's no doubt that something, or someone, is very dangerous, until we've been able to stop whatever it is, I'd be happier if I knew you were all safe. OK?' Sergeant Daniels' voice said this was more than just asking, it was a gentle order.

Sarah, Josh and Rupert all nodded their agreement, but Cassy seemed to be lost in her own thoughts.

'Cassy?' She just looked at him blankly for a moment. 'Did you hear me, Cassy?'

'Be careful Sergeant Daniels, something has changed.' She still had a faraway look on her face, almost as if she wasn't really paying attention.

'What's changed? And, how can you know that?' The sergeant asked.

'I don't know, but I can feel it.' Everyone looked at her questioningly, but she didn't add anything to this.

'OK. Look, I'm going to go now, check this story out and, as I said, I'll come back a little later. I think I will need to talk to you a bit more Cassy. James, Nadia, could I have a moment of your time?' Sergeant Daniels gave a sideways nod of his head to say he wanted to have a word in private.

'Of course.' Dad said as he looked at mum. They both followed him to the front door.

'I'm a little worried about Cassy. She seems to be acting oddly, and says she knows more than she could know. Any idea what it's all about?' He asked.

'Only that she's been having a lot of dreams over the last two nights and seems convinced that they're real. She wakes calling or even screaming, but doesn't seem to be frightened by them. I'm at a loss Peter.' Dad said. Mum seemed to be keeping very quiet, but did have a worried look on her face.

'Nadia, anything you feel you can add?' Daniels asked.

'No, not really.' She replied.

'Not really? Does that mean there is something?'

'What if her dreams really are some sort of, prophesy? I mean, could it be she really is learning about, whatever this thing is?' She had the same faraway look on her face as Cassy did, deep in thought, but also worry.

'I, I really don't see how that could be. If you want my opinion, I think she's got a very active imagination and thinks she's helping. But it's very dangerous ground she's walking here, or at least, it could well be.' Daniels was frowning as he spoke, obviously quite confused at her answer.

Dad put his arm around her, and as she looked at him, he smiled, but it was a smile that was for comfort. He felt she was obviously very worried, but he also felt she knew something he didn't, something she wasn't too keen to share.

'Look, at least until we've taken a look, can I ask you to make sure you keep her in. Josh, Sarah and Rupert too, or if they go home, ask their parents to keep them inside, just for now.' Daniels asked, but it was a friendly, strong ask, as if to say there was little choice.

'Of course.' Dad replied.

Police search

Sergeant Daniels sat in his car for a couple of minutes after leaving the house. There was something about Cassy which seemed different; he had known the Pride family for about ten years now, Cassy had been just a baby when he met them and he'd never seen her act like this before. Of course, she'd experienced quite a frightening thing, obviously, but seeing monsters, dreams telling her about the monster, it all seemed a bit farfetched to him. On top of that, she seemed to be remarkably calm about the bodies, Rupert had been the only one to look really shocked by it all, although Josh and Sarah had seemed much quieter than usual. Still, she and her friends have reported the bodies, so it was his duty to look for them and see if he can work out what's happened.

He called the station and asked for four or five police officers to assist him, if enough were available. He thought that, just in case, they had better search the woods as much as possible. He also suggested getting forensics there as they were investigating the report of bodies. Cassy claimed that the monster was at the clearing, so just to be thorough, he thought they had better take a close look, see if there was any evidence of anything there.

He waited in the car until the officers turned up, which wasn't long, it was a quiet town which didn't put a high demand on the police there so they were able to drop what they were doing to help. He gave them a quick account of what the kids had said and where they were to look first.

The officers entered the woods on the path that Cassy and her friends said they had found one of the bodies on. Once in, they spread out a bit to widen the search. It wasn't too long before they came upon the first victim. True to the description given by Cassy, the corpse was dried up like Shane Mc Adams' was, the comment about it being damaged was a bit of an understatement. There was a broken piece of a branch sticking out of it and the skin was torn in many places, including the face. Sergeant Daniels looked up, above there were a few broken branches, evidence of the body having been dropped from a height, it seemed from what he could see that it hit a few branches on its way down.

He shuddered slightly, what could have done this? Cassy's insistence that there was a monster passed through his thoughts, then the comment from Gracie O'Neil that the Devil had risen from the ground at the clearing, where Cassy believed the monster was. He shook his head as if to clear the crazy thoughts out. Then Cassy's words 'be careful Sergeant Daniels, something has changed' made him go cold. 'No, it can't be.' He said to himself, but accidentally out loud.

'Sarge?' PC Hughes, who was standing beside him asked in a confused way.

'What? Oh nothing, just thinking about something someone said. It doesn't matter. What do you make of this?'

'Well Sir, truth be told, I'm lost for an explanation. It looks like he was dropped from above, something must have dragged him up into the tree, then I guess lost grip and it fell. But a leopard is the only thing I can think of that could do that, and there's none of those about in England.' Hughes said, then thought about it for a moment. 'Unless there's been an escape from a zoo, or one that's been kept as a pet or something.'

'Good thought Hughes, might be worth looking into when we get back. It does seem certain that the body was dropped, but after being dried out going by the lack of blood. The question is, how would a leopard dry its prey out like this? OK, call in will you, find out how long forensics are going to be. We need to continue our search; the report is that there's three more bodies at the clearing.' Sergeant Daniels said. He then knelt down to see if there was any identification on him, but he couldn't find anything.

The walk to the clearing was eventless, there was nothing out of the ordinary. Sergeant Daniels looked at the trees as he passed, every now and then stopping to carefully examine random trees. A part of him wanted to find signs of a big cat, or any other predator, but there was nothing. He had carefully checked the trees near the other body, especially the one which the body must have fallen from, but there was no sign at all of any claw marks, which surely a big cat would have left, especially on the tree it climbed up with an adult human body.

The clearing seemed to suddenly appear in front of him, but his concentration on the trees and the thoughts which ran through his head had taken most of his attention. At first glance there was nothing out of the ordinary, he walked to the centre of the clearing towards the area where a fireplace had been built. Then an officer called out. 'Sarge, over here.'

Turning towards the officer, Daniels called. 'What have you found?' He didn't really need to ask, he'd been told by Cassy and her friend what it was, but he hoped they were wrong and the answer from the officer might have been something a bit less horrible.

'The other three bodies Sir, just like you said.'

He jogged over to the edge of the clearing to where the bodies lay. Judging from the clothing there were two women and one man. Might have been two couples and the first body they found had run, but from what? More to the point, from how many? To have killed three people and then caught up with the fourth, who had run, this had to be a few, there's no other possible way to have caught the fourth otherwise, was there?

Sergeant Daniels and one other officer crouched down to take a closer look at the bodies, the three remaining officers started to look closely at the area in hopes of finding something which might offer up a clue. None of them noticed a movement from the centre of the clearing as they were concentrating on the sides of the area. A shadowy type darkness started to rise from the ground, as black as the darkest night apart from its eyes, which burned like red fire.

Once it had risen from the ground and standing about as tall as some of the trees, it looked around. It could sense people about but couldn't locate them. The light was uncomfortable, but it was not at full strength just yet. Another few feeds, the life essence of just a few more would allow it to venture out into the day light, it was about half way there.

One of the officers turned as he took the whole area in, then he saw it, the huge towering darkness, he looked up and saw the eyes. A state of sheer terror struck him and as it did, the demons eyes grew bright, like the fires of Hell burned in them. He tried to scream, but all that came out was a strangled squeak.

'Davies, what the…' said another officer as he turned towards his fellow policeman, but the sight before him cut his words off for a moment. 'Sarge, everyone, RUN!' He yelled.

The others turned, and as they saw the monstrous thing before them so the fear struck their hearts. The demon seemed to suddenly be sent into action, its huge hand swept down and picked up PC Davies. It held him in front of its face and opened its mouth. It didn't put Davies in its mouth, but instead it seemed to suck. From Davies flowed a hazy, slightly glowing, red, vaporous flow which went straight into the demon's mouth. Moments later, maybe just ten seconds, it dropped the now dead officer to the ground. He was as dried out as all the other victims, unrecognisable now, other than his uniform.

Sergeant Daniels and two others had already fled, calling to each other to run as fast as they could. Daniels had called on them to split up, that way there was a chance of them getting out of the woods. But one officer had frozen in fear, he felt the sickening dread rise in his throat, his heart thumped so hard in his chest it felt like it might burst out, but his legs refused to move. Rooted to the spot by fear, he didn't stand a chance. The demon's huge hand swept down again and picked him up. He tried to scream but his throat was so tight nothing happened, it was as useless as his legs had become.

Once the empty body of the second officer was dropped to the floor the demon roared with the power it felt building up inside it. The scent of fear was still in the air, but it felt a confusion, for usually they went together, it's the pack instinct to stay together. This gave the demon an advantage, for a group was easy to follow, but now they had separated, it wasn't sure which way to go. It chose to take the path, this was the route these humans usually took, and fear had definitely gone that way.

Sergeant Daniels was running as fast as he could go, he'd always been something of a runner. He'd been a keen footballer in his youth and early twenties, however, his career as a policeman had taken him away from the game. He'd always liked the thrill of a fast sprint, but he'd never thought that it would be his only chance of survival as it was now. He'd been the one to run the main path, ordering the other two to take a different route. He'd yelled at them to spread out as wide as they could so that they were as far from each other as possible, that way at least there was a chance of two getting out if not all of them. Of course, he hadn't actually said this, in fact he'd used very few words, he'd also not checked to see if anyone had disobeyed him by following him.

Soon after he'd left the clearing, he'd heard a noise that chilled him to the bone, what he could only imagine was the monsters' roar. Other sounds he heard was what he thought must have been it starting to chase after them. It had filled him with one of those horrible feelings, like a twist in the stomach you can also feel in your throat. The sort of feeling where you just want to rip it out, but of course you can't as it's a part of you.

At every step he felt like it could be his last one, but then he heard it, so close behind him, the sounds of it chasing him seemed to get closer with every step he took. But then, it was huge, one of its steps were equal to ten of his, he didn't stand a chance, this he now knew. In his knowledge that he was about to die, to fall victim of this thing from Hell, he hoped that at least he'd given the other officers the chance they needed to get free.

He hadn't realised that he'd gone so far until suddenly, so it seemed, just ahead of him was the forensic team working the area around the body. 'Run, run now.' Was all he was able to get out before he reached them. He didn't slow down, instead he jumped, clearing the body on the floor and the woman who was on her knees on the other side of the body. As he'd called, she'd looked up at him, as had the others, but the dark mass that chased him had been all they'd really noticed. They had turned to run, but the woman at the body's side, kneeling down didn't have time to get up, and her fear sealed her fate.

Sergeant Daniels broke free of the woodland, but his fear didn't let him stop at that, he continued to run until he reached the other side of the field, where the path led up onto the pavement. Finally, he stopped, gasping for breath, his lungs eagerly sucking in big breaths of air, which never seemed enough. His legs felt wobbly and barely able to hold his weight up any more and his body was shaking with the fear. Leaning on the fence post to steady himself he chanced a look behind him. There were three members of the forensic team running towards him along the path. Fortunately, no demon from Hell was to be seen.

'What...? How...? Where...?' Came the babbled, unfinished questions as the first of the forensic team reached him.

Sergeant Daniels tried to answer, but he couldn't hold enough breath to manage one just yet, so he just held up a hand. His body was beginning to feel too heavy for his legs so, before he collapsed, he sat himself down.

It was about a minute later before he was able to get his words out, by which time the rest of the forensic team had caught up. 'Did all your team get out?' He asked.

They all looked at each other. 'Where's Alison? Where's Allie?' One of the team started to shout.

'I don't know. She was working on the body.' Another said in a defensive way. 'I haven't seen her since we ran. What was that? It was huge, it was… it was…' But he couldn't find any word to say what he wanted to say.

'This Alison, she was the one kneeling by the body?' Sergeant Daniels asked.

'Yes, yes, where is she?' The one asking after her demanded.

'I don't know, but I have a feeling, if she's not out by now…' He didn't finish the sentence. 'I've certainly just lost one of my team, probably two.' He said, although he was more thinking out aloud than talking to the others.

He then reached into his pocket and got out his phone, having called up the contact list, he called one of the other officers who ran a different way, but there was no answer. He tried the number of the other officer, but he didn't get an answer from him either. In the meantime, the distressed man from forensics tried to go back, but was held by the other two.

'Peter, what happened? You Alright?' Sergeant Daniels turned around to see James and Nadia coming over. 'Cassy and her friends were watching the woods from the upstairs window, she said she saw you get here and then you seemed to collapse. What happened Peter? Are you OK?' James asked, full of concern.

All Sergeant Daniels could say at this point was, 'Cassy's right, there's a monster in the woods.'

Mum and dad had stayed outside with Sergeant Daniels until he got a call from the other two officers who'd fled in different direction. Although in a state of shock, they were physically alright, but having witnessed one of their team being killed and knew what had happened to the second, their minds were a mess. Sergeant Daniels himself wasn't in a much better state, at least not to start with. Never had this small, sleepy town experienced anything like this before, but then, had anywhere?

The forensic team were likewise in a state of shock, especially the one who'd asked, and asserted his need to know about the woman, Alison. It turned out that they were a lot more than just work partners, but a husband-and-wife team. He was devastated and despite the obvious danger of returning to find her, he still tried to do so. The ambulance had been called and he was sedated for his own sake.

Sergeant Daniels had ordered an immediate cordon around the woods and strict "No admission" notices put up at every entry point. It was only after all this that he went back to the Pride household to talk to Cassy and the kids, but this time, he wasn't going to doubt their word.

He sat at the kitchen table with Cassy, Sarah, Rupert and Josh, meanwhile mum made them all drinks. Dad stayed with them, intrigued to find out what had happened as he had only caught bits and pieces. His friend Peter was a rational man, not prone to being nervy or exaggerate a situation, so to be this shaken up, something really serious must have happened. The drinks were served and mum sat next to Cassy and waited for the Sergeant to lead the conversation.

After about a minute of silence, Sergeant Daniels looked up, before this he'd just been looking at the mug of coffee in front of him. 'OK, can any of you give me any idea what we're dealing with in the woods? Cassy?' He asked. He knew it was a bit of a silly question as he was sure they would have told him before anyone got hurt, or indeed killed, nevertheless he had to say something, and he wasn't thinking very clearly.

'All I know is, Cassy's talked about a monster there and we found some dead people.' Josh said in reply. 'But really, I don't know anything else. Don't think Rupert or Sarah does either.' He added.

'You sound like you're blaming Cassy, Josh, it's not her fault.' Sarah argued in Cassy's defence.

'I wasn't blaming her. Honest Cassy.' Josh said, looking pleadingly from Sarah to Cassy.

Cassy seemed to be in a trance, she didn't look like she was paying any attention to what was being said at all. Rupert was also very quiet, although he looked like he was deliberately trying to avoid being noticed. Mrs Pride had called their parents and Rupert was worried that he was going to be in trouble, despite Mrs Pride assuring them all that they weren't.

'Cassy?' Sergeant Daniels said, as a means to get her to say something, but also a little concerned at her lack of, well, anything really.

Cassy looked up at him, her face had a look of someone lost in thought. 'I don't really know anything. It's just, my dreams are trying to tell me something but I don't know what. Yet.' She then looked down again, as if a great sadness had taken over her and she couldn't bear to have her face seen.

'OK, then can you tell me about your dreams. I know you've told me some bits, but tell me everything.'

Cassy didn't respond, her mind was far away, she was lost in her own thoughts.

'Hey sweetheart, I think it could help. You do seem to know something about all this, how I don't know, but you warned Sergeant Daniels before he left. I think we need to understand.' Dad said, using his gentle, understanding voice.

Cassy looked up at him. Mum put her hand on her arm in a comforting way. 'Your dreams, and thoughts about them might help.' She added in encouragement.

'In my dreams it chases me, always seems to be chasing me.' She stressed the me before a few seconds' silence. 'There are always people about, they're frightened, terrified and the monster gets them as it passes. I see it pick them up sometimes, but don't see anything else but there are dried up bodies everywhere,' she paused and looked at her friends 'like the ones we saw in the woods.' She then faced down again, occasionally looking up at the sergeant. 'Everyone's so afraid, but for some reason, I'm not, not for myself anyway. It keeps calling saying it's going to get me.'

'That sounds terrifying darling, it's no wonder you're not sleeping well.' Mum said, a look of concern on her face.

'I think it's after me. I'm the one it wants.' Cassy said to mum, looking her straight in the eye.

'Why would it be after you, Cassy?' Dad asked.

'I don't know. I'm just a young girl, a nobody.' As she said 'a nobody', a flash of sadness spread across her face.

'You are not a nobody Cassy, don't you ever let anyone make you think that.' Dad said, sounding a little cross, but not at Cassy.

'Far from it.' Mum added, with a faraway look on her face.

Sergeant Daniels' phone rang, he looked at the screen and then excused himself while he stepped aside to answer it. Mum and dad both put an arm around Cassy for comfort.

'You're my best friend.' Sarah said.

'And mine.' Both Josh and Rupert agreed.

'That makes you a very special someone to us.' Sarah finished.

Mum and dad smiled at them, nodding approvingly.

'I know, I didn't mean it like that.' Cassy defended, but there was something in her voice that said she wasn't being completely honest.

'I'm going to have to get back to the station in a few. Is there anything else you can tell me Cassy? Any of you? Anything at all.' Sergeant Daniels asked as he came back into the kitchen-diner.

'I think it can only come out at night or in the shade of the woods, like it needs the darkness. But maybe that's what's changing. It feels…' Cassy paused; she just didn't know what she wanted to say. She knew her feelings, but didn't know how to describe them, or what they meant.

'It feels, what?' Sergeant Daniels urged.

'More dangerous.' Was all Cassy could say.

'More dangerous? How? In what way?'

'I don't know. I just, somehow, I can feel it.' She looked every bit as confused as the sergeant did.

He decided that pushing it now was not a good idea, especially as he wasn't really feeling too patient, with the shock he'd just felt in the woods he might just get angry when he shouldn't. 'OK. I've got to go, there's a detective at the station who wants me to catch him up on the case. Listen Cassy, if anything comes to you, dreams or anything else, please let me know, your dad can call me. Is that alright?' Cassy nodded. 'OK, thank you.' With that, he turned to leave, and dad went with him to let him out.

Dreaming riddles

The rest of the day had been fairly eventless, Rupert, Josh and Sarah had gone home some thirty minutes after Sergeant Daniels had left. Sarah's dad had been the first to turn up, then Josh's mum had come soon after Sarah had left and she had taken Rupert too. There were no angry words, only words of concern and comfort.

Sarah had called Cassy a couple of times on their mobiles, otherwise they texted each other when they had their privacy. Josh and Rupert had also texted her and Sarah, but a lot of those messages were pretty much the same, questions about how monsters could really exist, how could Cassy know so much about it, and why would she be dreaming of it?

Mum and dad, although dad mainly, had had a number of talks with her, hoping to find a way to get her to talk about it all, and especially her dreams, more deeply. But she couldn't really remember any more than she'd told. She didn't know how to describe her feelings, although to her they seemed to make sense, she wouldn't be able to find words to describe them. Also, there was the fact that they were feelings, not thoughts, and feelings can often be strong but vague and therefore escape the description of words.

There had been no further news, or contact, from Sergeant Daniels and the day had seemed to drag on, although she had to admit, dinner time came around fairly quickly; maybe it was the evening that dragged most and just felt like the whole day. It was now nine o'clock and she decided to go to bed, she excused herself saying she was tired and then kissed mum and dad goodnight.

Having used the bathroom and changed into her nightie she paused at the window, just looking out. After a few moments she sat on the windowsill and just stared out into the darkness in the direction of the woods. Cloud covered the sky now; the frost had gone and the air had warmed up a bit, not too much, but then it was only January, but it was so much warmer than the morning had been. Nevertheless, it was very dark outside and there wasn't anything to see, but Cassy stared out into the darkness anyway.

Inside her, what felt like deep in her stomach, she had a feeling, a dread maybe, but it's meaning was just out of reach. Like an itch you can't reach to scratch, this was a feeling she couldn't quite clear in her mind. One thing that was clear was that she wasn't able to see anything outside so, as she was tired, she moved over to her bed and got in. She wrapped the quilt around her, unsure if it was for warmth or comfort, and then closed her eyes. A couple of minutes later she was asleep.

She stepped out of the school cloakroom and into a field, for a moment she frowned as there isn't any field at the school.

'Hey, wait for us.' Came the familiar voice of Rupert, she turned to see not only him but Sarah and Josh too.

She replied, but somehow didn't speak, like she'd thought it. As they caught up with her, she turned back the way she had been facing and there in front of her was the woods. They only seemed to take a couple of steps before they were in the woods which was now dark, like night time. This didn't seem to bother them and they played games, hide and seek, and tag. But then, a shadow loomed over them, despite the darkness which now seemed to have lightened a bit. She looked up and there were two red eyes, quite dim, but then Rupert screeched as he saw it and those eyes glowed brightly and the monster started to move towards him while it bent to grab him.

'Run Rupert, Run.' She called, but somehow her voice was silent. 'RUN.' She screamed, but again there was no sound even though she'd put all she could into it.

She screamed again, trying even harder. Although her scream was silent, Sarah looked in the direction she was looking, just as Rupert was picked up by the monster. Anger filled her up, she wasn't afraid, but she was mad. Sarah, on the other hand was terrified and her scream was loud. Like it had been fuel for a fire, the monsters eyes glowed even brighter, and then even more so when Josh saw it and the fear hit him. She tried to call out again, trying to get them to run, but she couldn't make a sound. It was then that it picked up Sarah and Josh, and as it had done to Rupert, it sucked them dry.

After it finished with them it started to look around, but couldn't seem to spot her below it. It said, in a deep voice which almost crackled with evil. 'I will get you Cassy Pride, you're mine.'

Cassy woke up as dad came into her bedroom. 'Cassy, are you OK? Bad dreams again?' He asked as he reached her bed and gave her a hug.

Cassy turned to look at the clock, it was a quarter to ten, she'd only been in bed for about half an hour. Looking back at dad again she nodded. 'I'm OK, thank you dad.' She said in reply to his concerned questions.

'What was it about this time. The same as the others?' He asked, hoping it would be the right time to get her to talk about it.

'Yeah, but…' She frowned for a few seconds. Dad just looked at her, eyebrows slightly raised, he didn't say anything. 'This time Sarah, Josh and Rupert were taken by it.'

'Oh sweetheart, that's awful, but they're safe at home. I can understand it's very disturbing for you, but it is just a dream.' He said trying to be comforting.

'Cassy darling, are you alright?' Mum said from the doorway.

Cassy just nodded and gave a small smile. 'She's just said in this dream it took, Josh, Rupert and Sarah.' Dad volunteered on her behalf.

'Oh darling. Are you OK?' Mum asked compassionately.

'I'm OK, thanks for coming in, dad.' She said as she lay down again. 'I am tired though.'

Dad leaned over and gave her a kiss. 'OK sweetheart, but I'll come back if you have any more. Got to make sure my favourite girl is OK. Alright?'

'OK dad.' She smiled. At that, dad and mum left her to go back to sleep.

She sent Sarah a text just asking her to text back, she then lay there for a while waiting for the text but just thinking about the dream. Sarah didn't take long to text back and asked if everything was OK. Cassy replied it was and she just had a dream that spooked her. Sleep took over again soon after.

Then, she was skipping down the road feeling happy. She kicked a coke can which took to the air with ease before hitting a town notice board, something made her want to go over and see what was on it, so she did. There was a full page from a newspaper there, in big letters it read, "The demon claims its fourteenth victim", the rest of the page was blank. She frowned, 'I stay in every night, so it can't get me.' She said to herself, but out aloud.

She turned to continue her journey but standing behind her was the dark black mass that was the monster. She looked at it as it looked at her, the fire in its eyes were not bright and it didn't seem to be able to actually see her even though it was looking at her.

'I can smell you; I can taste you Cassy Pride.' Came its deep, crackling voice. It was then that a flicker of fear struck her, and the monster's eyes glowed bright. 'I can see you now.' It said as a huge hand swished downwards in an arc to grab her.

She jumped to the side and somehow, despite the hand being enormous, it missed her. She ran as fast as she could down the street. It was only then that she realised that the town seemed empty, certainly there was no one in the streets. Her thoughts went to Sarah, Josh and Rupert. A deeply hidden memory flashed in her mind, a memory of her friends dying in the woods. She then smiled inwardly, 'that was a dream I had' she thought to herself.

As she ran faster than she thought she could, she came to the town centre, an old part of town where they had kept its old traditional look. It was an open space with the ground of stone slabs and a small fountain in the centre. It was only then that she realised it was day time, and the sun was shining making it a bright day. She stopped, suddenly struck by the thought. The monster was out in the light. In her dream she knew this was wrong, the monster could only be out at night, or where it's protected by shade.

Suddenly, a deep roar came from behind her, so deep, so loud, so terrifying. She turned, the monster's face was inches away from her, she couldn't help it but a cross between a screech and a scream erupted from her. Its mouth opened wide and she felt herself being sucked in. She felt its touch on her shoulders and she struggled frantically to get free. 'Get off me, get off me.' She yelled at it, but it made no difference. As everything went dark, its deep, crackly voice said. 'Now I've got you Cassy Pride.'

She suddenly opened her eyes and sat up, dad who had been trying to wake her got head butted, fortunately not too seriously. Cassy put a hand to her forehead where the contact with dad had happened, he did likewise.

'Sweetheart, are you OK? That was quite a bump.' He asked. She didn't answer, just nodded and she fixed her gaze forward looking somewhat stunned. 'These dreams of yours are getting worse. You've never headbutted me before.' He smiled to let her know the last part was meant to be mildly humorous.

'Sorry dad.' Was all she said.

Dad gave her a hug. 'Do you want to talk about it?' He offered.

Cassy didn't respond straight away but looked down at her bedding while she tried to get her thoughts in order. That last dream had shaken her more than any of the other ones had. 'Dad?'

He looked at her, but she wasn't looking at him. 'What is it?' He asked.

'If this monster *is* after me, is it possible that my dreams are… I don't know, maybe trying to guide me somehow?' It was then she looked up at him.

'To be honest sweetheart, I don't know what to make of any of this. Monsters don't exist, yet there's one in the woods. I guess, anything's possible.' As he spoke, he moved himself up to sit next to her.

'Dad, is there a notebook, pad or something I could have? I think it might be a good idea to write my dreams down, at least some bits of the dream.'

'You know, I think that would be a good idea. If nothing else it'll help you to focus on them.' He smiled at her. 'Tell you what, I'll go and have a look, have you got a pen or do you want me to get you one?'

'Yes please, I mean, I'd like a pen please.'

As dad left her room, she looked at the clock, it was nearly quarter to one. She checked her phone in case Sarah had tried to text her, but nothing showed. She felt a fidgety feeling, like she had to do something, but this was mixed with a feeling of dread, a pit in her stomach that ached. The frustration inside her was confusing, she felt like she had answers, but no questions, these were being delivered by her dreams, they were telling her something, if only she could understand what.

'Here we go.' Cassy had been so lost in her thoughts that his voice made her jump a little when he came back into her bedroom. 'Sorry, didn't mean to startle you.' He then held a notebook up. 'Hope this is

OK, it's only a small one, but should be big enough, at least for now. Tell you what, how about tomorrow we see if we can pick up a bigger one in town.'

'This'll be fine. Thanks, dad.' She said as he handed it to her.

'Let's hope that was the last dream of the night eh. I am getting a bit worried about you.' With that he leant over and kissed her on the forehead.

'Does if make me weird if I said I hope I do have more tonight?' She asked, looking at him awkwardly.

'You wake up screaming, calling and shouting "get off me" and you want more?' Dad looked at her with raised eyebrows. 'What on earth for Cassy? Why would you want more? They're terrifying you.'

'That's the strange thing, I'm not frightened by them, I'm not even frightened in my dreams. OK, the last one was a bit scary, but most of them, I'm honestly not scared. But I know they're trying to tell me something. Maybe, the more I have the better I'll be able to understand them.'

'Back to your question, maybe a little weird.' He grinned at her so she knew he wasn't being serious. 'Listen, I think tomorrow it would be a good idea if we can set aside some time to really discuss it. The dreams, how they make you feel etc. You're waking up in a panic, shouting things, but say you're not scared. You know, I think I would be.' Cassy didn't respond, there was nothing she could find to respond with so she just nodded with a smile. 'Try and get some sleep now, OK.'

'Night dad.'

'Goodnight sweetheart, sleep tight.' He blew her a kiss from the bedroom door before leaving the room.

As soon as he'd left, she opened up the notebook and, holding the pen ready to write she thought about the dream, the parts that she thought might be important. There were the fiery eyes that seemed to get brighter before it attacks. It was after her. It couldn't come out in the light, but then it did in the last dream. Did it seem bigger? She thought of the newspaper page, blank apart from the headline about the demon claiming fourteen victims; was that important? She made a note of each of these points before putting the pad on her bedside table, turning the light out and then lying down.

She lay there in the dark; sleep didn't seem to want to take over and her mind was full of thoughts about her dreams. Deep in her mind she felt there was something she was missing and she went round and round the points she'd written. It didn't seem to matter how many times she went over them, or thought about the dreams in detail, nothing was helping her to find whatever might be missing, but the feeling was there nevertheless.

It took a little while before she fell asleep again and sometime after she did, the dreams started, but this time it was a bit different. It was the strange feeling that came first, like she was as light as a feather, floating. She opened her eyes and found herself looking down at Woodhaven. To her right was the woodland which seemed much bigger than she thought it would be, all around the town were huge hills but the ground that the town sat on was a flat area at the bottom of them.

As she looked down, studying the town from her high point in the sky, she felt like a guardian angel, watching and protecting the people there, it made her smile. It was then her eyes caught sight of the dark mass, moving slowly, watching carefully for its next victim. She tried to concentrate on getting a better view as she was so high up, and as she did, she began to float down towards the ground. Then, all of a sudden, she was travelling at great speed, flying through the air so fast the ground almost seemed to appear in front of her. She stopped suddenly in what felt like a couple of inches and found herself face to face with herself. But it was her from her last dream.

She frowned, trying to understand how this could be, but then her thoughts went to the monster, she had seen it from way up high. She turned, but didn't actually move, it was almost like she was able to look at what she was thinking about. The monster was looking down at her, her other self, but it wasn't seeing her. Its eyes were quite dull, the flames just flickered. She looked back at herself and realised that time was going slowly as if everything was in super slow motion. Her face started to change expression, from thoughtful to afraid. She looked back at the monster which also moved slowly and its eyes started to brighten. As soon as they were a bright glow it said 'I can see you now...'

As if she had been pulled with huge force, she was travelling back up into the sky. The speed was such that she watched the ground become distant very quickly. She struggled to get back down, to help herself, to see if anything was important, but she couldn't, she had no control. Then all of a sudden, she was looking up at the ceiling in her bedroom. It was getting light and she was sweaty. Her body didn't seem to want to move and she questioned if she was awake or in a dream.

She lay there not moving, unable to move, for some time. Then she took in a deep breath, held it for a few seconds and then let it out. She looked at the clock, it said it was seven fifty-three. She frowned, it felt like she had only just fallen asleep. Sitting up, she reached for her note pad, but couldn't think what to write. In this dream she had been high up, flew down, seen the monster's eyes glow and then flew back up. She wrote that down, but what else? There had to be something more to it, but what?

Cassy got out of bed and put on her dressing gown then, taking hold of the pad and pen, she went down stairs.

'Good morning Cassy.' Mum said as she walked to the kitchen table.

'Morning.' She replied, but her thoughts were elsewhere.

'How are you feeling this morning? You didn't seem to have any more dreams last night, at least, none that made you…' Mum paused while she tried to think of a way to put it. '… well, call out.' Cassy didn't reply, instead she just frowned, looking at the note pad which was closed. 'Cassy? You, OK?' Mum asked, her words showing her concern.

'Yes, sorry, I'm fine.'

'And dreams? Did you have any more?'

'I did have one. It was strange, can I tell you about it when dad's here? Where is he anyway?' She asked.

'He's a bit tired. I think all your dreams have tired him out, so he's having a bit of a lie in.'

She looked up at mum, her face had the look of guilt. 'I'm sorry mum, I've been a nuisance. I'm not trying to be, honest.'

Mum walked over to her and gave her a hug. 'Nonsense darling. You're having a difficult time, that's not your fault. Families stick together and support each other, that's nothing to beat yourself up about.'

'Yes but…' Cassy began, but mum stopped her.

'Both your dad and I are happy to support you with this, and besides…' She paused for a second or two. '…I think you're very important to this whole business. And, somehow, I believe you hold the key to sorting this whole mess out, I'm certainly proud to be by your side on it.'

She looked up at mum, frowning. 'You're proud of me?' She asked looking a bit surprised.

'Yes, of course I am. Of you, how brave you are, how caring you are and I'm proud to be your mum.' Mum looked sincere.

Cassy threw her arms around mum's neck and gave her a hug. 'Thank you.' She said, and for a moment she had to fight to hold the tears in.

New cases, new danger

Cassy sat at the kitchen table, she hadn't been hungry so didn't have a proper breakfast, mum had given her a couple of slices of toast and jam, but she only ate one slice. She had then cleared the table and, with her note pad open she had read over what she had written and tried to add more, but the harder she thought about it the less sense it all seemed to make. She then got a drawing book she had and was sat there making a brain-storming diagram in the hopes of getting somewhere with it all. Mum stood, leaning against the kitchen cupboard, watching her work. She smiled as she couldn't help but think how she looked like a young student studying for university.

It was nearly nine-thirty before dad came down. He was about to apologise for being in bed so late when mum put her finger to her lips and gave a silent shsh before pointing at Cassy. Dad looked at her working away at the table and smiled. He walked quietly over to the kitchen, as he neared the kettle the doorbell rang. Dad raised his eyebrows and shrugged his shoulders with a smile. 'I'll get it.' He said putting the kettle on as he spoke.

'Oh, hi dad.' Cassy greeted. 'Didn't hear you come down.' She added.

'Morning sweetheart.' He returned while heading for the door, he took the route past Cassy and kissed her on the cheek as he passed.

It was Sergeant Daniels at the door. 'Morning Peter, this is becoming a habit.' He greeted cheerfully with a smile, but the smile quickly faded when he noticed the strained look on his face. 'What's happened?' He added.

'Can I come in?' Sergeant Daniels asked in a voice that was flat and weary.

'Yes, yes of course. Please.' Dad said as he stepped aside giving a welcoming hand movement as a further invite. 'What's wrong?' He asked.

He didn't answer straight away, instead he walked through to the kitchen. He looked tired, worried and maybe even slightly in shock.

'Morning Peter.' Mum said, but on seeing the look on his face she moved over to the table and pulled out a chair for him to sit on. 'Please sit. What's up? Has something else happened?'

'It's getting worse.' Was all he said to start with, he then looked down and slowly shook his head as if he couldn't quite believe what he was about to tell them.

Cassy looked at him and her face became very serious. She wanted to say something, take a guess at what the sergeant was about to say, but resisted. Mum looked at her, her face asking what it was she was thinking, but Cassy barely noticed. Everyone looked at the policeman, waiting for him to speak.

'I mentioned yesterday, before I left here, that there was a detective who wanted to take over the investigation.' Sergeant Daniels said in a very distracted way.

'Yes, well something about wanting you to fill him in on the case I think it was.' Dad agreed.

'Yes, yeah, well anyway, he thought I was nuts, or pulling a prank, or something. He didn't take my story seriously anyway, at least, not the monster bit. We had already started to put police tape, warning not to cross the line, at every entry point to the woods. He had sent a team of armed officers in to get the bodies out and decided to station officers at the main entry paths for the night. Although shocked by the state of the bodies, he still didn't accept my conclusion about some huge monster being there, so he decided to join the officers overnight.' He then fell quiet.

While he had been talking, mum had made him, and dad, a coffee. She put them on the table as he went quiet. Everyone looked at him, wondering what was coming. 'What is it Peter?' Mum asked. 'What's happened?'

Sergeant Daniels looked up; he barely noticed the coffee and so didn't thank her. 'At about two o'clock, the monster attacked them. Some officers escaped and made it back to the station where they called me. They had heard a disturbance from the officers guarding the entrance further along but hadn't managed to get them on the radio. Then, it attacked their group. The detective was one of those it caught. Altogether, we lost…'

'Oh my god, oh no.' Cassy said as she stared ahead at nothing in particular.

'Cassy?' Dad said as an invite to carry on, but she just frowned, deep in thought.

In her mind she was adding up how many had died so far. 'Six have been killed up to the end of yesterday, right?' She said.

Eight I think, yes, yes eight.' Sergeant Daniels said. 'Shane McAdams, the four you kids found, two of my officers and the lady from forensics. Why?'

'And it took six last night?' Cassy asked, but perhaps more as a statement than a question.

Sergeant Daniels looked at her in surprise, mouth slightly open. 'Cassy, how could you possibly have known that? Your dreams?'

'She's right then, it was six?' Dad asked the sergeant, who nodded.

'Six police officers?' Mum asked in a voice that said she was having difficulty believing it.

Cassy puffed out a breath as if she was having difficulty breathing.

'Sweetheart, what's wrong?' Dad asked sounding worried.

'Darling?' Mum added

'Oh my god.' She repeated. 'That makes fourteen altogether.'

Mum moved closer to her and put an arm around her shoulder. 'I know darling, it's terrible, so many deaths and here of all places.'

Cassy looked up at mum, then at dad, then at Sergeant Daniels. Her face had a deep troubled look and she had flushed slightly. 'You don't understand.' She then looked at the note pad and the paper she had been drawing on, she pointed at the notes she'd made and in particularly the bit about it claiming fourteen victims. 'I dreamt it last night, there's something important about fourteen victims.'

Cassy stood up and began pacing the room as she thought. 'I've been trying to understand it. Two of my dreams seemed to be, I don't know, like the same thing only in the first...' She stopped as she tried to remember how it went. '...I was walking, then I kicked something, a can, I think. It hit the cupboard thing in town, you know where people put adverts and stuff.'

'The town notice board?' Sergeant Daniels asked, but in a helpful way.

'Yes, anyway I went over to it and there was a piece of paper, no, it was a page of the newspaper… I think, it's a bit fuzzy now.' She put her hand to her forehead and closed her eyes tight as she thought. 'Yes, it was from the newspaper, it said the monster had claimed its fourteenth victim.' She moved to the table and looked at her notes again. 'No, the demon, not monster. I turned and it was right behind me. It then chased me to the centre of town, you know where it looks all old fashioned, and then it caught me. That's when I headbutted you, dad.' Strange under the circumstances, but she couldn't help a bit of a smile at the thought.

'Ah, yes, that I do remember, that explains why you were screaming 'get off me.'' Dad added. 'How, I mean, is the number fourteen important then?'

'I think it must be. I'm sorry, I'm trying, it's just hard to remember. I wrote down what I thought was important, the points I could remember.'

Dad moved to her and gave her a gentle hug. 'It's OK sweetheart, we'll work through it, together, OK.'

'Cassy, you said you had two dreams that were the same, or something.' Sergeant Daniels said as a prompt.

'Yes, only in the second one I was high up in the sky looking down at myself and the demon. Then I flew down and was close to myself and it, like I was a different me. I'm confused about what it means because I was looking from me to it. Its eyes were burning but not bright, they then became bright flames before it started chasing me. I didn't see anything else because I was flown back up, high above it all and then woke up. By that time, it was morning and I got up. But I know it all means something, I just… I don't know what.'

'OK, let's go through it carefully, maybe we'll figure something out as we go along. You said you were looking down at yourself and the monster, demon from high up, right? Sergeant Daniels said helpfully.

'Wait, that's right, I was looking at it, it was light, it was daytime. That's it, perhaps after fourteen victims it can come out in the day. Maybe that's what the newspaper was trying to tell me.' Cassy spoke the last part quickly, in an excited voice, but the excitement was anything but happy and her face was one of dread.

Sergeant Daniels looked at her, then at her mum and dad, he had a look of deep dread on his face. 'How can we beat it if it can come out in the day now. There might be no stopping it.'

'There's something else too.' Cassy said before picking up her note pad again and looking at it. 'I think it was bigger in this dream.'

'A though has just come to me,' Mum said, she frowned and there was a thoughtful delay before she carried on. She then looked at

Cassy. 'you've said more than once that in your dreams it's after you, but you're not afraid. Why? Do you know?'

'I don't know. Maybe it's only after me because they're my dreams, I don't know if that's really so in real life.' As she spoke, she realised that she didn't really believe that, she felt sure that it was after her for some reason.

'Well, from what you've said before, you do seem to think it is after you, but even if it is just in your dreams, do you know why you're not afraid of it. I know dreams can be… well, strange sweetheart, but just maybe, there's something important about you not being frightened in your dreams.' Dad added, hoping to get some more information from her.

Sergeant Daniels looked at Cassy, his face was very serious. 'Yesterday you said how everyone was frightened, many were being caught, but you only felt afraid for them. I don't understand that. What I mean is, if it was just a dream, nothing really means anything, but if these dreams are somehow true, no I mean, if they are some sort of reality, what is it about you that stops you being afraid.'

Cassy looked at him for a few seconds, confused, she then looked at dad as if to ask for help. 'Umm.' But she didn't know how else to react.

'I think Peter, Sergeant Daniels is just asking the same basic question, can you think of why the monster, demon thing doesn't frighten you in your dreams.' Dad said trying to clarify.

'I don't know, I'm trying to understand it all.' She replied, but was starting to feel frustrated and her voice was beginning to sound it too.

'Darling, it'll come to you.' Mum said trying to be reassuring. 'Be patient, we'll be there to help you.'

'In three nights, fourteen people have died. If it can do that not leaving the woods, imagine what it could do if it went into town, during the day.' Sergeant Daniels was sounding more than shocked, or recovering from the night before, he was now sounding impatient and fed up. He looked at everyone wide eyed. 'We haven't got time to be patient.'

'Peter, it's not Cassy's, fault. She's trying to help, and has given more information than anyone else. If patience is what's needed then it's what we need to give.' Dad said defensively and somewhat crossly.

'Yes but…' Sergeant Daniels began.

'No buts Peter, she can't do better than her best.' Mum said putting a hand on Cassy's shoulder. 'Getting angry is only going to slow things down.'

'I'm sorry. I lost friends last night; things are getting worse and the town looks to me for answers. This is the first time since becoming a police officer, I haven't got a clue what to do.' He looked at Cassy who looked worried, like she was in trouble. 'I'm sorry Cassy, you've been really helpful, I know it's not your fault.'

Cassy was about to reply but dad got in first. 'Look, Peter, it's been very stressful. Why don't you go home and get some rest, if you can, we'll let you know if something comes up.'

'Wish I could, but I've got to head off to the station.'

'Sergeant Daniels…' Cassy said in a gentle voice, then paused until he was looking at her. '… I'll keep trying, I promise. I need to know why it's me it wants and why I'm dreaming about it so much too.'

Sergeant Daniels forced a smile and nodded, he then stood up. 'I'd better go. Please, let me know if you get anything else. Anything, something that could help stop this thing.'

Cassy's phone rang, she quickly checked to see who it was, then seeing it was Sarah she picked it up. 'I will, I promise.' She said to the sergeant before taking her phone out of the room. 'Hey Sarah.' She said on answering it.

'Cassy, have you heard the news. Everyone's talking about it. They're saying there's a beast in the woods. Cassy, it killed some cops last night.' She spoke fast and in an excited voice.

'I know, Sergeant Daniels has just been here. How does everyone know so soon?' Cassy asked.

'Some boys saw it, they saw the monster attack a group of cops by the playground, everyone's starting to panic. They're planning to go into town and demand something is done.'

'Hang on.' She said to Sarah, then rushed back into the kitchen. 'Dad, has he left yet?' She asked, her voice sounding urgent.

'Literally just walked out, why?' Dad answered.

'Call him back, please, it's important.' Although spoken like a demand, she really meant it as asking.

Mum had already started to respond and was nearly at the door. She opened it and almost at the same time called. 'Peter.'

Sergeant Daniels stopped and turned. 'Everything OK?' He asked.

'Cassy...' she began, but Cassy stopped her as she pushed between mum and the door frame. 'I think there's a panic about to start in town. Some boys saw what happened last night and it's spread through town.'

'How do you know this, your friends on the phone?' He asked.

'Yes, Sarah's just said.'

Sergeant Daniels turned back and walked to the house again. 'Thank you, good girl.' He said to her. 'Can I talk to her?' He added.

Cassy held her phone up to her ear again. 'Do you mind telling Sergeant Daniels what you told me, Sarah?'

'Yeah, sure.' She said.

Cassy handed him her phone. As soon as he took it, a dizzy spell hit her, like a pressure in her head that built until it felt like a headache. The air turned a sort of bluey/grey colour and hundreds of little lights filled her vision, swirling around in a random way, in all directions. She closed her eyes, but all that did was to turn the bluey/grey into black, the lights carried on their dance. The dizziness built up until she felt like she was rocking, she opened her eyes and her balance gave way.

Images flowed through her mind, like a hundred small clips of different films all jumbled together, but they were not films. She tried to see them more clearly, but they seemed to go so fast she couldn't really make any sense of them. Slowly, she began to feel her body again and a slight pain began in her right shoulder. Her head began to thump in rhythm with her heart, like a pressure that came and went inside her, and voices, so distant she couldn't make any sense of them. The images started to slow down and she realised they were more like still photographs, like a slide show of a photo album, but still going fairly quickly on a computer screen.

'Cassy, Cassy, are you OK?' Said the voices, but she couldn't quite make out if it was mum, dad, Sergeant Daniel, or all of them together. Then, she opened her eyes. Sergeant Daniels was kneeling down beside her and mum and dad were rushing over. She looked up at the ceiling, her mind was a jumble for a few seconds and she couldn't make any sense of what was happening. She took in a deep breath.

'Sweetheart, are you OK?' She heard dad ask.

'Darling, what happened?' Mum asked when she saw Cassy's eyes open.

'I... I...' She didn't know herself and couldn't think of anything to say. Her mind was still very confused, like she had a head full of clouds.

'It's OK Cassy, you just fainted. Are you hurt?' Sergeant Daniels asked.

Cassy sat up, she still felt a bit dizzy, the pressure in her head was starting to fade but still felt like a headache, although it didn't exactly hurt. She put her hand to her shoulder. 'I think I hurt my shoulder.' She said, she wanted to say it wasn't bad, but somehow, she couldn't manage it, like she had no strength left to speak.

Mum knelt beside her. 'Let me take a look, just in case. You gave us quite a scare for a moment then. Come on, let's get you into the living room.'

Cassy nodded, she felt so tired, like all the energy had been drained from her body. A flash back to her dream where the demon started to suck the life from her flashed through her mind, and she realised that that was how she felt now. As mum and dad helped support her as she walked through to the living room another dizzy spell struck her, but it wasn't as serious and didn't last for more than a few seconds. 'How long was I… on the floor?' She asked.

'You fainted, but was only out for a second or two, but you did scare us for a moment.' Mum said. She gave a reassuring smile while she opened Cassy's dressing gown and slipped her nighty off her right shoulder. 'It's a little pink but you haven't broken the skin. Let's hope it doesn't bruise.' She said taking a close look.

Sergeant Daniels stayed in the kitchen area to speak with Sarah while mum and dad took care of Cassy in the living room.

Cassy and the fear demon

Sergeant Daniels hadn't stayed after talking to Sarah on the phone. In fact, the chat was only very brief, then he handed the phone back to dad and made a quick exit, wishing Cassy well as he went and apologising for his rather hasty departure.

Mum and dad had said Cassy should stay on the sofa until she felt a hundred percent again. Although it didn't take long to get over the faint, there remained an unease inside her. Thoughts came to her in the form of images in her mind and she couldn't shake the feeling that she was in need of doing something, but, a bit like her dreams, that something was just out of her reach to understand.

Soon after Sergeant Daniels left, Sarah had come over, concerned about Cassy, he'd told her that she had fainted and as this had never happened to Cassy before she was worried about her friend. She had also called Josh who said he would tell Rupert. It wasn't long before all four friends were together in Cassy's home. To start with mum and dad weren't sure about it, thinking that Cassy would be better off being kept quiet, but she was so insistent that she was OK it was probably less stressful to let it be.

Cassy explained what the Sergeant had told them, and also how parts of her dreams were coming true.

'So, you knew that fourteen people had been killed before Sergeant Daniels told you?' Sarah asked, but her voice said it was more of a surprised thinking out aloud.

'Well, not really. Not until he started to tell us about what happened and then it was…' Cassy began, but couldn't think how to put it.

'It was?' Josh said, trying to urge an answer from her.

'My dream, I dreamt the demon had got fourteen people. I just, I thought it must have been.' She said sounding defensive.

'What's going to happen next Cassy?' Rupert asked, he couldn't help a small nervous but excited quaver in his voice.

'I don't know, I'm not a… thingy Rupert.' The three friends looked at her, Josh and Sarah couldn't help a teasing smile. 'You know, what are they called? People who tell the future.' She said feeling a little embarrassed, and perhaps just a little frustrated.

'A prophet or a seer.' Mum said from the doorway. 'But listen kids, Cassy doesn't need lots of questions just now. She had a faint and could do with a more relaxed time, yeah?' Although 'yeah' was spoken as a question, it was more of a polite, gentle, don't do it. 'Look, why don't I get you lot a drink of something, eh.'

'Yes please mum, can I have a coke?' Cassy gave her a cheeky grin. Although mum did let her have coke, it was more of a treat than a regular drink.

'OK, what about you three.'

'Same for me please, Mrs Pride.' Sarah said.

'Me too please.' 'And me. Please.' Josh and Rupert said almost together.

Mum smiled and turned towards the kitchen to get them all one.

Sergeant Daniels got back to the police station in the town centre. A short time later, crowds of towns people started gathering, there were lots of worried, fearful faces there. Some of the men were grouping together as one of them was calling for a mob style attack on the thing in the woods. As the shouts started to become an uproar, Sergeant Daniels stepped outside to try and quieten things down a bit. On seeing him, the crowd turned to him, men and women alike started to shout demanding questions. 'What are you going to do about it?' 'How many have to be killed before we do something?' 'We not safe, the police are supposed to protect us.' 'Why aren't you out there doing something?' 'We demand justice for those who have been killed.' Etcetera, etcetera. They were getting quite angry.

Sergeant Daniels made his way to the centre of the square and stood on the edge of the fountain so he was raised up from the people in order to be seen. 'Please, everyone, please calm down. We *are* doing everything we can.' He called out, stressing the word, 'are'. But the people started muttering, not really believing him. 'Please, you all know me, you know I would never let something like this go. I'm doing all I can to try and find a way to beat it.' He added.

'What exactly is it?' One man called out.

'Someone said it was a monster, or something.' A woman said.

'Don't be daft, Marg, this isn't fantasy. It's some sort of escaped beast.' Her husband said.

'Must be a bear.' Shouted another.

'The police have the bodies; can't you tell from them what's doing this?' Called another.

'That's my boy you're talking about, not some piece of meat, show some respect can't you.' Came the tearful, but angry pleas from Rose McAdams, the first victim's mum.

'We don't know what it is yet, we know it's big, we know it can move quickly, but as of yet, what it is, is a mystery.' Sergeant Daniels said, unsure of how he should even start trying to explain.

'So, what are we supposed to do? Sit around and wait until it comes for us?' Someone shouted, anger clear in his voice.

'Firstly, it's important to try and remain calm. We have put tape up around the woodland entrances and ask everyone not to cross it. For your own sakes, please don't. I suggest that while we, the police, try and catch, or destroy whatever is doing this, you let us do our job. Big gatherings, in this medieval mob way is not going to sort it out.

So far it hasn't left the woods as far as we can tell, but to be on the safe side, I advise everyone to stay indoors as much as possible. No hunting parties.' He stressed the last part, making it an official warning.

Another round of uncontrolled shouting began. Other police officers came over to try and help calm the situation down, but this had a limited effect. All officers had been ordered to keep what they knew to themselves, especially those who had actually witnessed the demon. More panic would only run the risk of costing more lives.

Deep in the woods, at the clearing, the dark shadowy demon rose from the ground. The air was filled with the scent of fear, or something close, it could sense that this came from many people. It's target, the one known as Cassy Pride could be among them. If not, could she resist trying to help? The demon raised its head so its nose was in the air, it sniffed as it slowly turned until it had fixed where the scent came from. If the fear wasn't strong yet, one look at its monstrous form would surely fill their hearts with terror. More to feed from, more strength to gain, more power to destroy its unwary enemy, Cassy Pride.

It looked in the direction of the scent and then the path the humans had fled on, and then it began its journey towards the town, and the people there. It made its way through the trees, its body, able to pass through those which would otherwise get in the way, like a smoky mist that goes around them, but solid once on the other side. As it moved it could sense the feast which awaited it, and its whole body was filled with the anticipated excitement. Unable to keep it in, the demon roared, and like a thunder clap, it filled the air.

Back at the Pride's house, Cassy sensed it, although she didn't understand what she was feeling. What flowed through her was a dread that made her heart beat faster, but as oddly as her dreams, she didn't feel it as fear.

Mum and dad were in the kitchen when a noise, a little like thunder but not quite, filled the air outside. Dad looked out of the window to see if the sky looked like a thunder storm was brewing, but the cloud cover was light. Then, from the living room came the sound of concerned calls to Cassy from her friends. Dad was the first to get in there followed directly by mum. Cassy was sitting like a statue, her face was blank, her eyes wide in a stare, but she didn't seem to be looking at anything in particular.

'Cassy, what's wrong sweetheart?' Dad asked sounding a little panicky as he rushed over to her. Cassy didn't seem to be aware of anything and didn't answer, or indeed move.

'She just… went like that.' Rupert said.

'She sat up and started staring like she is now, just before the thunder came.' Sarah added.

Mum rushed over and knelt down in front of her. 'Cassy, Cassy, can you hear me?'

In Cassy's mind she could feel the demon, almost see it. The roar had been like her warning that it was coming to get her. She felt a strange buzzy sort of feeling run through her and her mind seem to talk to her, but almost as if it was from someone else. The words weren't really clear, more a hazy mumble, but she understood the meaning. It was up to her to face the demon, she had to brave this monster. Then, as if a switch had been pressed, Cassy relaxed her body from the statue like way she had been sitting. It took a second or two before she seemed to focus her eyes on mum, but when she did her face said that all was not well.

'What's wrong? Are you alright?' Mum asked.

'It's coming. Did you hear it call?' She said, ignoring mum's question.

'The demon?' Dad asked, but Cassy just looked at him, blankly. 'Do you mean that thunder was the demon calling, some sort of roar?'

'I have to go to it.' She said, her voice was quiet, almost as if she wasn't really talking to anyone but thinking out aloud.

'No, absolutely not.' Dad said with a tone that left no choice, this was an order, a demand that was given with total seriousness.

Mum's face took on a look of dread, almost as if deep inside her she knew Cassy was right. But although she would never allow her daughter to walk into such a dangerous situation, she had a look that said it might not be their choice.

Cassy looked at dad, then at mum followed by each of her friends in turn. 'You don't understand, it's after me.' She said, slowly shaking her head as if to make her point stronger.

Before she could get any further, dad took hold of her by the arms. 'That's why you're not leaving this house. Sweetheart, it will kill you just like the others.'

'Please darling, don't do it.' Mum pleaded. Dad looked at her, confused, as she made it sound like they had no choice in Cassy's decision. Mum's eyes were wet as tears pooled in them.

Cassy lowered her head, deep inside she could feel a pressure build up in her chest, like the dread was filling her up with hopeless need. She felt like she was going to burst. She slumped into the sofa like she had given up. Sarah came and sat beside her. 'It's so dangerous Cassy, let Sergeant Daniels do it. He is the grown up in charge.' She said, trying to be helpful.

'Yeah, we're just kids, what can we do?' Rupert said backing Sarah up. Josh nodded in a way that was a cross between agreeing with his friends and a gentle means to back the argument up.

Cassy looked at her friends, a sad smile that looked like defeat washed over her face, this along with a slow blink of her eyes made everyone relax a bit.

'OK, you kids stay with her.' Dad said, then looking at mum added. 'I'm going to give Peter a call, tell him what Cassy has just said, just in case.'

Mum nodded in agreement, then stood up and followed him out of the room. Once in the hallway and by the phone she looked at dad, a deepened look of sorrowful worry covered her face and the tears which had wetted her eyes began running down her cheeks. Dad took hold of her, hugging her closely. 'Hey, we've got to be strong for Cassy. I can't...' he paused while he tried to find the right words, '...don't understand what's happening to her, but we have to have faith that it'll be over soon.'

'What if she's right?' Mum said.

'If it's after her, then even more reason to be strong for her.' Mum nodded as if in agreement, but she walked away, heading for the kitchen as if she wasn't really meaning that.

As dad tried to call Sergeant Daniels, Cassy said she was going to go upstairs to get dressed. She then walked out of the living room with a look of almost being in a trance. Her mind was running wild with thoughts she couldn't understand, it was starting to drive her crazy with frustration.

'You, OK?' Dad asked as she passed.

'Yeah, going to get dressed.' She replied. Mum smiled at her as she passed through the kitchen.

A few minutes later she came back down, fully dressed, coat on and with trainers on her feet.

'And where do you think you're going?' Mum said, not really as a question but more of a challenge. Dad, who was now with her looked at Cassy with suspicion.

'I just need some fresh air; I feel a little sick. I'm only going to stand out the front.' She answered.

'We'll be watching, we're only looking out for you. We're worried that's all.' Dad said, adding to mum's challenge.

'It's OK.' Cassy reassured, and then asked. 'Did you talk to Sergeant Daniels?

'No, I can't get him, just keeps ringing. He must be out. I'll try again in a few.' Dad answered.

Cassy nodded, then she went into the living room. She got close to her friends. 'I have to go. It's crazy, I know, but a lot of people will die if I don't.' Cassy whispered so mum and dad didn't hear. 'I've told mum and dad that I'm just going to stand outside to get some air.' She didn't wait for a reply, instead she headed towards the front door.

'Cassy.' Sarah said in a hushed whisper, but Cassy didn't reply or even look back. Sarah, Josh and Rupert just looked at each other with a questioning look on their faces. Then they followed her out.

Once outside, Cassy stopped and looked back at the kitchen window. She could see dad looking, she smiled a reassuring smile then turned her back on the house, lifted her head and took in a deep breath. Dad, satisfied that she was just getting a breath of fresh air turned back to mum. 'She's acting off, since she had that faint, she not been quite...' He scrunched his face up as if struggling to find the right description. '... I don't know, right.' Mum just seemed to be in something of a trace, deep in thought maybe, whatever, she didn't respond. 'Honey, you OK?'

She looked up at him. 'I'm afraid James.'

'Hey, it'll be OK.' Dad said sympathetically. 'We'll keep an eye on her. She'll be alright once this is over.'

'But what if...' But she didn't finish.

'What if what?' Dad asked.

Mum's face dropped as she looked out of the window, her eyes opened wide and she opened her mouth a bit, then screamed. 'CASSY, NOOO.'

Dad turned around to see what she was so worried about. The front gate was open and Rupert and Josh were just running out of sight, Sarah presumably ahead of them. As they disappeared out of sight, they heard Rupert call. 'Cassy, don't.'

The town square was getting louder as the people argued, shouts for the help they were now delaying were becoming more and more angry. Sergeant Daniels kept calling for the people to calm down, but the anger in them just kept on rising. The other officers were equally unable to calm thing down, even though they tried to move among the crowd. Then someone shouted 'what's that?' and pointed a finger in the direction of the woods, although the woods itself couldn't be seen for the buildings, especially the town hall.

'Is that a black cloud?' Someone else asked.

Fairly quickly a hush fell over the people as they looked. A dark form was moving towards them, it looked like smoke but much thicker, but it wasn't easy to see the shape, all that was seen was a part of the demon's head over the top of the large hall which stood between them and it. But this didn't last long, for it quickly became seen clearly, the demon was heading their way and wasn't far from them. As it came closer, it was clear that it was moving to the side of the hall making it easily seen, and terror filled the hearts of everyone.

The demon sensed the rising fear and it filled it with excitement and hunger, its eyes glowed brighter than ever before. It made a spine-chilling noise, a little like a roar but this noise crackled like electricity sparking. It came to the hall and stepped around it, and once in the square everyone panicked. Some ran, other were so terrified they couldn't move. Sergeant Daniels tried to call to the people but not only did words escape him, his throat was so tight he couldn't make a sound.

A little down the road which led into the old square, Cassy ran in their direction. Not far behind her was Sarah followed closely by Josh and Rupert. They saw the huge demon and were immediately struck with the same fear the other people felt, but they couldn't leave Cassy to run in there alone. What they really wanted to do was to stop her, she couldn't possibly stand any chance of doing anything against such a huge monster like that.

Once the demon was completely in the square and towered over the people, it spoke. 'Where is Cassy Pride?' Screams broke out as the booming voice filled their heads. 'I will have Cassy Pride.' It said after a pause.

The towns people started to rush in all directions again, no-one seemed to be trying to get anywhere in particular but panic made them run. The demon then reached down and grabbed the first person it touched, this was the school's lead bully, Jake. It stood up straight and lifted Jake up to its mouth. 'Feeding time then.' Its crackling voice said and Jake screamed in sheer terror.

Cassy was by now just entering the square, she looked up and saw the demon lift Jake up to its mouth. Inside her head flashes of images, she couldn't quite focus on flowed through her mind. Her body seemed to flush with a warmth she couldn't understand, she thought fear should make you feel cold, but this was a fleeting thought, there, and then gone almost at the same time. Then her dreams came back to her. She stopped running and came to a halt. Like the memory of the dreams came with an unseen set of instructions she suddenly understood. Its eyes glowed in the presence of fear, not just because it was about to chase. She could look at it without the eyes glowing bright because she didn't fear it in her dreams. It had been so obvious she was fearless but she failed to understand what it meant. If she could remain unafraid, she was invisible to it.

The warmth that flushed through her body started to tingle. For a moment she felt dizzy, her sight became a little hazy and the air took on a slight bluey haze. Hundreds of tiny, bright stars filled her sight, just as it had done about an hour ago when she fainted, but somehow this was different. She took in a deep breath and her head cleared; the tingle turned into a flow of what felt like a sort of electricity which touched every part of her body. She then realised that here she stood, in front of this monstrous thing, and although when she arrived her heart thumped heavily, she was now, just a couple of seconds later, free of all fear. How this could be she didn't know, and cared little, time was too short to worry about that. 'Let him go.' She demanded as loud as she could and walking towards it.

Her voice seemed to rise above the sound of all the other panic-stricken people, and suddenly a hush fell over the square and everyone looked at Cassy. The demon stopped, for this voice seemed to hold a promise. It lowered its hand to its side and turned. But it could not see who called.

'I am Cassy Pride, and I'm not scared of you.' She called.

Gasps sounded out among the crowd. This quiet, small, almost meek young girl now stood braver than the biggest man, challenging this huge demon which stood about thirteen to fourteen metres tall. Sarah reached her and tried to pull her away, Josh and a quaking Rupert arrived and tried to help. The demon saw them straight away, their fear, although they showed bravery, was plain to see. The demon made a throaty, growling sort of noise as it looked down at them.

'Don't be afraid.' Cassy said.

She then felt a flow of energy run through her again, instinctively she grabbed Sarah and Josh's hand, without knowing why, Josh grabbed Rupert's hand. As soon as they were all touching a small shock like flow of energy ran through them all which seemed to come from Cassy. It wasn't clear to any of them what it was, but then the demon roared and looked around.

Rupert was the first to notice, the fear in him had gone, now he felt strangely brave. Both Sarah and Josh felt it too. 'What's happened?' Sarah asked. But it was a question she seemed to ask herself.

'Move. Surround it.' Cassy said with an unusually masterful tone.

Without question or thought the three friends ran. Sarah went behind the demon, opposite Cassy, while Josh and Rupert went to either side of it. It wouldn't have worked any smoother if they had planned it and practiced until they got it perfect.

About this time, mum and dad entered the square, instant panic hit them on seeing Cassy so close to this enormous, terrifying black monster. This seemed stronger than the fear for themselves. They drew to a sudden stop, struck silent by the sight before them.

Cassy calmly looked up at the demon. At this point a slight glow began which spread and surrounded her, it was not bright, in fact it was only just visible, but it was there nevertheless. 'I am Cassy Pride.' She repeated. 'It's me you want, let him go.'

From behind her came a screech from mum and dad, they then called to her in what ended up as a loud whisper. 'Cassy, come away.'

The demon knew she spoke the truth, its prey was indeed here, but it couldn't see her which frustrated it, she should be terrified.

Now its attention had turned to its intended prey, it opened its hand and Jake fell. He dropped the four to five metres and landed on his feet, but the impact of such a fall broke his right leg. He ended up in a heap on the floor by the demon's foot. Sergeant Daniels ran to his aid, followed by another officer. As they did, Sergeant Daniels said 'Cassy, get away, now.' But she didn't seem to even notice them as she looked straight up at the demon. They quickly took a hold of Jake and moved him away. Fortunately, they managed this before the pain sunk in, and without being noticed by the monster that towered above them.

The demon searched for its prey, but it was unable to see her, although a faint glow it did see, like a ghostly echo of the young girl.

It bent towards it reaching out its huge hand, Cassy raised her arms so they would not be trapped as the demon picked her up. Gasps came from the crowd along with dread filled shouts as they watched, helpless, as this young girl met her fate.

Mum screamed 'CASSYYYY' as the hysteria at seeing her little girl being taken by this evil monstrosity grew. Dad called her name too and at the same time, for helpless despair had gripped them both.

The demon lifted her up until she was close to its mouth. 'Cassy Pride, I have you now.' It stated, the crackle of its voice almost vibrating with its victory; the demon then opened its mouth. Cassy felt her head swim, like it was in a whirlpool being turned round and round. Before her, she could see what looked like a stream of red vapour leave her body and go towards the demon's open mouth. She shook her head to try and clear it, then she felt an energy flow through her again. The stream of red vapour stopped, hovered for a moment and then sucked back into her. Instinctively, she held her hands out in front of her. A rush flowed through her, coming from her all parts of her body and into her arms, then a bright white beam flowed from her hands and into the demon's mouth.

The noise that came from the demon was partly a grunt, partly a scream, although deep in sound, and partly a muffled roar. It swayed slightly and, letting go of Cassy, brought its hands to its head as if it was going to explode.

Cassy fell, it was a drop of about twelve metres, a fall that, if it didn't kill her, it would leave her with many broken bones. She landed feet first, so many sounds of horror came from the people around, and uncontrolled sobs from mum and dad even though they were some distance away. As Cassy's feet touched the ground, her legs bent with the impact, she sank into a crouching position where her hands hit the floor to break the fall. To the sheer amazement of the crowd, and almost hysterical relief from mum and dad, she stood up, then moved to her original position.

The demon's body seemed to pulsate, distort as if something was trying to get out of it by pushing from the inside. It swayed for a few seconds before regaining some control of itself. A fury welled up inside it, a rage like it had never experienced. It looked towards Cassy, although it couldn't see her, and barely was able to see the hazy glow that surrounded her. It bent over and roared, from its mouth came a stream of flames, so hot it burned blue. To the utter despair of everyone in the square, the flames swallowed Cassy up, and she could not be seen in the jet of fire.

Mum collapsed as all the strength left her, all she was able to do was cry hopelessly, dad held on to her and his tears joined hers as they watched the flames burn their dear daughter alive. They were utterly helpless as she suffered the worst fate imaginable.

However, inside the stream of intense fire, Cassy stood, the flames ran around her like stream water around a rock, almost as if she was in a bubble. The heat couldn't even touch her. She held out her hands so they were straight in front of her and a white ball of energy formed from the palms of her hands, stretching from one to the other. She opened her arms out then the ball turned into a beam which was like a laser, bright and crisp clear. It ran from her to Rupert and Josh, who, without thinking or understanding, opened their arms in the same way Cassy had, Sarah did the same. The beam entered the fingers of the boys and through the other hand and to Sarah's, creating a square around the demon. The moment the square was complete, merely a fraction of a second later, the demon stopped its roar and the flames were gone, the beam then stopped. Gasps of sheer confused amazement broke out as Cassy stood, unharmed.

She then looked up at the demon, her eyes were focused, confident and full of warning, her face determined. 'I am Cassy Pride, and you don't frighten me.' She said, almost as a repeat of her earlier words. Then with a sudden movement she held her right hand out, palm forward and upwards. A beam of light, shot out of her palm hitting the demon in the chest, then she lifted her other hand, making a double beam. The demon roared in pain as the light struck. The beam held for a few seconds before it stopped. The demon swayed, it rocked, and the pulsing of its body increased, until, like a balloon filled with black powder which popped, it exploded. The smoky type make-up of its body spread out before being sucked in on itself and then it shot down to the ground and vanished for good. On the old stone which made up the road, there was left a black mark, it looked like a bag of black powder had been dropped and bust leaving an uneven edged circle.

For a few moments, there was utter silence, everyone just stared at Cassy with amazed wonder. Mum and dad got up and ran towards her as did Josh, Rupert and Sarah. Then someone shouted. 'Cassy Pride, our saviour.' Some started to chant her name, others chanted 'Hero.' Some even got it right and chanted 'Heroine.' But it made little difference, she was being celebrated regardless of what words were being used.

Then, a stunned silence fell over the crowd as Cassy's legs buckled. She felt all the energy had been taken from her body, her head span and thumped in time with her heart, which got slower and slower until it stopped. She didn't feel herself land on the floor with a thump, nor did she hear the change in the crowd's mood. In fact, she had barely heard anything as the feverish confusion had muffled everything.

Mum and dad reached her together, instantly falling to their knees. Dad checked, but she wasn't breathing, he then checked for a pulse and panic hit him when he couldn't find one. For the second time mum broke down, the worry, despair, relief, joy and then back to despair was just too much, her precious girl was gone, and all she could do was to cradle her in her arms.

Sarah, Josh and Rupert stood by them, tears filled their eyes, their minds almost a blank but desperately trying to find something to say, but there was nothing there. Mum took a hold of dad and they held each other tight. Sarah knelt down beside the body of the best friend she'd ever had. 'You saved us all. You showed us how to be brave.' She said.

Rupert and Josh knelt down too. 'Even me.' Rupert said between choked breaths.

'You're my hero Cassy.' Josh added tearfully.

Sarah then laid a hand on Cassy's upper chest. 'One in.' She said, Josh and Rupert lay their hands on top of Sarah's. 'All in.' The three friends said together. A small glow flowed down their arms, the remainder of the energy Cassy had passed to them, as it reached their hands it became a small but bright light that paused for a brief time at the point of contact between Sarah's hand and Cassy's chest, then it entered Cassy. Suddenly, she sat up while noisily sucking a huge lungful of air in.

'It's a miracle, she's a miracle.' Someone said, and the town erupted in cheers, laughter and joyous sounds, not even the shock of the terrifying events could dull it.

Sergeant Daniels, who had come over to offer support, placed a hand on mum and dad's shoulders, when they looked up at him, he smiled and gave a nod. It was the sort of nod that said, very clearly, "I'm so proud of her" without having to speak a word.

Cassy, who sat a little dazed for a few moments tried to get up, she was dizzy but with help made it to her feet.

'Cassy Pride.' A call came, making its way through the noise. The crowd fell quiet and people moved aside to reveal Jake. He was pale in the face and obviously in a lot of pain, but when Cassy looked at him, he said, 'I've been so horrible to you, never treated you nice, yet you saved my life risking yours. Why?'

'Everyone deserves a second chance?' Was all she said. Jake, not knowing how to respond to that, just nodded his thanks.

'C'mon, it's time to get you home.' Dad said smiling with pride and putting a hand on her shoulder.

Cassy put her arm around Sarah's shoulder for support as she was still feeling weak, Josh and Rupert playfully pushed each other to be the other one to support her. 'Take it in turns.' She said smiling and wrapping her arm around Rupert's shoulder, as he was closest. 'Do you know something?' She said to all of them, mum and dad included.

'What darling?' Mum said, still a little teary and shell shocked.

'That didn't feel so good. Remind me not to do it again.' She said, and then gave a little giggle. The three friends joined her giggling, and as they walked down the road towards home, mum and dad joined in too.

Cassy will return in

Cassy Pride and the witches four

Deep underground where a maze of caves met at a cavern, they wailed and the mournful sound travelled the dark passageways. They had failed, at least, their pet had. The one they made of darkness, hatred and torment had been defeated, fallen by the hand of the one it had sought to destroy. Their creation, their child as they saw it, the demon who hunted by taking advantage of the human instinct to feel fear, who grew strong by taking their life energy, the fear demon had gone.

For centuries, a millennium even, it had been the stuff of legend, to some, the Devil, to others Hell's demon, to others still, a monster who occasionally rises to feed on the unsuspecting people. In more recent times, however, it had left people's minds or become myth to those who heard of it. For it had been a long time since it had been called upon to do their bidding.

As their loss darkened their already dark hearts, so their anger grew, and as their anger grew, so did their need for revenge. The Master would no doubt punish their failure, he was the only one they feared, so they had to find a way to get their revenge, at least he might forgive them then. Their demon was powerful, but they were more so, perhaps their only choice was to face the light, to rise to the surface, to do the job themselves.

They had little need for spoken words, their minds were linked, they thought as one, and they started to plan. At least if they had a plan, the Master may be easy on them, but it had been so long since they last had to face the light on top. In any case, it was now up to them, they had to get it right, they had to make sure they succeeded, they had to defeat the enemy known as Cassy Pride.

About the author

B. J. Browne lives in a small coastal town of Aberaeron, West Wales.

He's spent years working with children and young people, at present he works as a Clinical Support worker, working nights. It is during this time he does most of his writing.

In his pastime he's a passionate environmentalist, a big fan of trees and all life. Enjoys a bit of gardening, playing with the dogs and entertaining his internal fantasy world where his stories grow and develop.

Coming soon

Cassy Pride and the witches four – Part two of the Cassy Pride trilogy.

When young eleven-year-old Cassy Pride hears screams from the woodland near her home, she finds herself compelled to investigate. While doing so, she encounters a huge monster, a demon, like a shadow that's blacker than black and with eyes of red fire. That night she's haunted by nightmares of the demon and its victims who have been sucked dry, this confuses her as she feels no fear, at least, not for herself. When, the following day, Sergeant Daniels, inform her and her parents that a young man was killed in the woods, Cassy knows what state the body is in and realises that her dreams are trying to tell her something.

Supported by her best friends, Sarah, Josh and Rupert, she plans to go to the woods the next day in search of answers. While there, they discover more bodies, all dried up like its first victim. Fleeing the woods, they report their findings to the sergeant who goes in to look, but while there they are attacked by the demon and two officers are killed along with a woman from forensics.

As fear grips the town and more people are taken, Cassy's dreams continue and she soon understands that the demon is there for her. But, Cassy holds a secret not even she's aware of, and so it's set for an exciting showdown that will change her life, permanently.